SPECIAL AGENTS
DEEP END

sam hutton

With special thanks to Allan Frewin Jones

HarperCollins *Children's Books*

First published in Great Britain by HarperCollins *Children's Books* 2003
HarperCollins *Children's Books* is a division of HarperCollins*Publishers* Ltd
77-85 Fulham Palace Road, Hammersmith, London W6 8JB

The HarperCollins *Children's Books website address is*
www.harpercollinschildrensbooks.co.uk

6

ISBN-13   978 0 00 714842 4
ISBN-10   0 00 714842 9

Text and series concept © Working Partners Limited 2003
Chapter illustrations by Tim Stevens

Printed and bound in England by Clays Ltd, St Ives plc

SPECIAL AGENTS
DEEP END

Also in the **SPECIAL AGENTS** series:

2 Final Shot
3 Countdown
4 Kiss and Kill
5 Full Throttle
6 Meltdown

Prologue

'Move it! You're fifteen seconds behind schedule! Come on!'

Speed was of the essence. They had to be in and out of the vault in less than ten minutes.

The heat in the confined space was oppressive. Nerves were stretched to their limits. The tension was intolerable.

There were five men down in the vaults of the Hatton Garden Diamond Depository. They were about to break in to the main room which contained thousands of priceless cut diamonds.

The hissing and flashing of a plasmacutter sent shadows flying.

The big man barking out instructions watched intently. 'Lenny – how long?' he demanded.

The man with the cutter paused and wiped his sweating forehead. 'One minute, Mr Stone. Just one more minute.' The door was made of thick steel bars and needed precision cutting. Beyond the door, a long, narrow room was filled with row after row of black boxes. Floor to ceiling.

'Not good enough! Make it faster!'

Another man spoke. 'Seven minutes.' He was looking at a stopwatch. Counting down. The gang had to be out of there in six minutes, fifty-five... There was no margin for error.

Another man crouched against the wall, his fingers flying over a laptop. Cables led to an electronic wall-panel.

Michael Stone's hand rested on the man's shoulder. 'John?'

Like all the others, John was sweating freely and running on pure adrenaline. 'I'm almost there,' he said. 'Almost.'

Michael Stone's eyes turned to the last man. He wore a headset. The man nodded. 'All clear so far, Mr Stone.'

A black van was waiting round the corner, a clump

of darkness in the deserted pre-dawn streets. In the driver's seat, the lookout rubbed his eyes, peering anxiously into the gloom. The waiting was almost unbearable.

Lenny let out a gasp of relief as the cutter severed the last bar. The heavy door tipped forwards and went crashing to the floor. The noise was deafening. Lenny cut the torch. For a moment everything stopped dead. In the sudden silence, each of them could hear their own thundering heartbeat.

'Six minutes!' The countdown was relentless.

Stone stepped into the strongroom, scanning the rows of black boxes with a wild light in his eyes. He turned.

'John, it's up to you now!'

'OK, boss.' John's fingers skidded over the keyboard. Numbers whirled on the display screen. John wiped his damp fingers on his shirt. This was it. This was the moment. All eyes were on him.

He punched a finger down on the ENTER key, and then came the sound of six hundred electronic security locks releasing themselves in sequence. The front panels of the black boxes opened in a long dark ripple that ran around the room like a Mexican wave.

Michael Stone spread his arms in triumph. 'It's pay day, boys,' he said.

The gang surged forwards. Heavy black bags were unfurled. Hands lifted the trays of diamonds down from the boxes. The contents sparkled and flashed as they cascaded into the bags.

Michael Stone watched silently. There was no doubt in his mind that he was about to walk off with twenty-five million pounds' worth of gemstones.

'Five minutes!'

A crazy, feverish energy filled the men as they scooped handfuls of diamonds into the black bags. Everything had worked perfectly. Just a few more minutes and they would be gone.

The link to the street was still open. Suddenly a shout burst through the earpiece of the contact man's headset. It took a split second for him to register what he was hearing. Then he let out a yell. 'Police!' he screamed, scrambling to his feet. 'They've got Ray!'

Michael Stone's eyes went dead. Around him, his well-drilled team fell apart as each man raced for the stairway out of the underground vault.

But there was no escape. A floodtide of police officers poured down the stairs to cut off their escape route. The battle was brief and brutal. The gang were soon subdued, handcuffed and cautioned.

Throughout the struggle, Michael Stone did not

move a muscle. He just stood there, ankle-deep in diamonds, watching his plans crumble around him.

A grey-haired man stopped in front of him and calmly began to speak. 'Michael Stone, I am arresting you for burglary at the Diamond Depository, Hatton Garden, at 03:40 hours on Wednesday 16th July. You do not have to say anything. However, it may harm your defence if you fail to mention, when questioned, anything you later rely on in court. Anything you do say may be given in evidence.'

Michael Stone looked at Detective Chief Superintendent Jack Cooper. He smiled grimly. 'I've made you wait a long time to say that to me, haven't I, Superintendent Cooper?'

The detective nodded sharply. 'It was worth the wait, Mr Stone... believe me, it was worth the wait.' He turned on his heel and left his officers to finish the arrest.

Michael Stone had been right. It had taken DCS Jack Cooper five years of concentrated effort to finally pin him down. But it was worth every moment. With Stone behind bars, organised crime in London would lose one of its most deadly masterminds.

Cooper climbed the stairs up to ground level. Ahead of him lay the inevitable press conference and the gruelling interviews for breakfast television.

'Mum! I can't find a clean leotard!' Maddie Cooper's voice rang along the hallway from her bedroom.

Her mother came to the kitchen door. She grinned at her daughter's usual early-morning panic. 'Have you looked in the airing cupboard?'

Maddie's flushed face appeared around her door. Her long blonde hair was falling into her eyes. 'Oh, right... thanks!'

Frowning, Maddie bounded along the corridor to the airing cupboard. It was hard enough getting herself organised first thing in the morning without her mother making things worse by being helpful.

She burst into the kitchen, stuffing a black leotard into her Royal Ballet School backpack.

'Food!' her mother said, pointing to a stack of toast.

'No time,' Maddie said. She took the leotard out again to make sure her tights were in there, too.

Her mother was sitting at the kitchen table, half-watching the morning news on the portable TV. 'What time are they picking you up?' she asked.

Maddie glanced at the wall clock. 'Right now!' She snatched up a piece of toast and ran out again. She had just remembered something else that she needed from her bedroom.

A shout from her mother stopped her in her tracks. 'Maddie! Quick. It's your dad!'

Maddie was back in the kitchen in an instant. She leaned across the table, her eyes wide, mouth half-open.

On the screen, she saw a press conference taking place. There was a scrum of reporters. Extending microphones and bulky video cameras pointed towards Maddie's father. He looked hot and uncomfortable under the blazing lights.

'Good morning, ladies and gentlemen,' he began. Maddie sank into a chair. It sounded so weird to hear her father's voice coming out of the TV. She had realised he was on a major case – he'd been on virtually permanent overtime for months now – but she hadn't expected anything as big as this. 'Do you know what it's all about?' she breathed.

'Yes, I think so,' her mum replied. 'Shush!'

'I am going to read you a prepared statement.' Maddie's father looked down at a sheet of paper. 'In the early hours of this morning, working on information received from reliable sources, a squad of officers from the Metropolitan Police apprehended a gang of intruders at the Diamond Depository in Hatton Garden, London. The gang had broken into the main vault and were in the process of removing a large quantity of diamonds when they were arrested. They are all currently being held in custody, pending formal charges.'

Superintendent Cooper looked up. 'I am now in a position to tell you that one of the men detained is Michael Stone, Managing Director of the security firm, Stonecor.'

A ripple of interest ran through the throng. Cameras flashed.

Maddie's mother clapped her hands together. 'Well done, Jack!' she shouted gleefully at the TV. 'You got him!'

'He's finally nailed Michael Stone?' Maddie gasped. 'Wow! Way to go, Dad!' Although her father tried not to bring his work home, Maddie knew that he had been preoccupied with that East End businessman for almost as long as she could remember.

Her father's statement continued with details of the criminals who were caught in the act of plundering the diamond vault.

Maddie hardly heard a word. She was gazing at her father with a mixture of pride and elation. As a child, her great ambition had been to join the police and work alongside him. But then she'd discovered ballet – and her interest in chasing criminals had taken a back seat. But that didn't stop her revelling in her father's triumph.

'I can now answer your questions,' Jack Cooper said, looking as if that was the last thing in the world that he wanted to do.

A chorus of questions erupted. At the same moment, the intercom buzzed.

Maddie leaped across the room. 'Yes? Hello?'

'Your ride to school is here.' It was the voice of Mario, the doorman to the Coopers' apartment block.

'Can you ask them to come up, please? My dad's on the TV.'

'I know,' came Mario's voice. 'I'm watching him. It's about time someone got that Stone guy off the streets. I'll send them up.'

'Thanks.'

Within minutes Maddie's tall classmate, Laura Petrie, was in the Coopers' kitchen, alongside her mother. Both of them were staring at the TV, completely caught up in the excitement of the moment.

The report had briefly moved to a piece on Michael Stone. It showed him as the respectable, successful businessman, as the proud family man and as the well-known face around the clubs and restaurants of the West End.

'And all the while,' said the voice-over, 'under this facade of respectability, Michael Stone was believed to be at the head of a criminal empire that stretched across Europe.'

'Didn't I tell you Dad was on to something big?' Maddie said to Laura, her voice bubbling with excitement. 'It's got to be such a buzz when you bring down a big villain like Michael Stone.'

Laura laughed. 'A bigger buzz than dancing the lead in *Giselle*?'

It was Maddie's turn to laugh. 'Almost!' she said.

It was Laura's mother who finally broke the spell. She glanced at the clock. 'Oh, my goodness! Look at the time. We're going to be so late.'

It was half past eight already. They had to be in White Lodge in Richmond Park in less than half an hour. Miss Treeves, the girls' dance mistress, did not tolerate lateness. She often told them how privileged they were to be pupils at the Royal Ballet School, and how such a privilege demanded the highest standards of self-discipline, dedication and punctuality. 'Ballet is the highest form of art and deserves to be taken seriously,' she would often say.

Maddie could do a good impersonation of Miss Treeves in full flow, although making fun of the brittle old lady was a perilous pastime!

Maddie found it hard to take life completely seriously, especially when everything was such fun. Her dancing was going so well that Maddie had been chosen to appear on stage next week at the Royal Opera House in Covent Garden, dancing as the third cygnet in a charity presentation of *Swan Lake*. It was enough to make her head spin just to think about it. And she wasn't even sixteen yet! Maddie grinned. Now that her father had slammed the door on Michael Stone, there was no fear of him missing her performance.

All things considered, Maddie thought as she jumped up into Mrs Petrie's Range Rover, life couldn't get much better.

❌

'Could you see me properly from where you were sitting?' Maddie asked her parents as they walked out through the Royal Opera House stage door and into the street. 'Did you have a good view of everything?'

'We saw you perfectly,' said her father. 'If you want my opinion, you were the best dancer in the entire show. I thought you were absolutely brilliant.'

'Da-ad!' Maddie's face was split by a huge grin. 'Hardly!'

'You were wonderful, sweetheart,' said her mother, 'and I'm very proud of you.'

The Charity Gala performance of *Swan Lake* was an opportunity for the school's most promising pupils to dance on stage with the Royal Ballet Company itself. Maddie had risen to the challenge with all her heart. Not surprisingly, she had felt nervous for days beforehand, but once she had stepped on to that huge stage with the music in her ears, all her doubts had fallen away.

The audience was long gone and the auditorium lights had dimmed. It had taken Maddie ages to drag herself away from the party in the dancers' dressing rooms. Her parents had waited patiently, fully aware of how much this meant to their talented daughter.

With her mother on one arm and her father on the other, Maddie stepped out into the warm, starlit night, her feet hardly touching the ground. The magical evening wasn't over yet: her father was treating her to dinner at Bertorelli's in Floral Street.

The restaurant was just across the road, but first they were going to drop Maddie's backpack off in the car. They headed towards the car park.

Maddie couldn't stop smiling. She knew that she was on the brink of a wonderful future. All she had to do was to reach out and close her fingers around it and the world would be hers. In September she would enter her final year at White Lodge, then, at sixteen, would move on to the Upper School in Covent Garden to complete her training. After that, Maddie could hardly bear to hope that she might be asked to join the Royal Ballet Company itself.

Suddenly a figure moved out of the shadows. Maddie caught the movement in the corner of her eye. She turned her head, sensing that there was something wrong. Horribly wrong.

The man had no face. Where his features should have been, there was just a blackness. He's wearing a mask, Maddie thought. Why?

She felt a sudden tension in her father's hand. The faceless man's arm rose, and Maddie heard her father call out a warning as he lurched forward.

Everything seemed to happen in slow motion. A succession of dull thuds burst into the air. Her father's body twisted as he tried to protect his wife and daughter. Maddie felt her mother's hand slide from her arm. Something hit her in the side and sent her spinning around. She crashed to the pavement, stunned and helpless, staring up into the black sky.

As Maddie lay there, the masked man murmured over her head, 'Goodnight – from Mr Stone.' Then he turned and melted back into the shadows.

A kind of quietness descended. It seemed almost

peaceful to Maddie as she lay there. There was no pain, although she understood in a vague way that she had been injured. She felt herself drifting. She wondered what had happened to her parents. She hoped they were all right.

She wished she could feel her legs.

She closed her eyes.

She could hear strangers bustling around her.

The next sound she heard was the wail of a siren getting gradually nearer.

Good, she thought.

Now everything would be OK.

✪

TOP LONDON POLICE OFFICER AND FAMILY
IN SHOOTING OUTRAGE

Detective Chief Superintendent Jack Cooper, his wife and daughter were ruthlessly gunned down last night as they left the Royal Opera House in London. A massive manhunt is underway to catch the lone gunman, who had apparently been waiting for them to emerge from the building.

Only minutes before the

tragedy, Jack and Eloise Cooper had been watching their fifteen-year-old daughter, Madeleine, dancing on stage. The masked gunman quickly disappeared from the scene, leaving his injured victims lying on the pavement. Police and ambulances arrived at the scene within minutes, but they were too late to save Mrs Cooper, who had died instantly under the hail of automatic pistol-fire. Superintendent Cooper and his daughter both sustained serious injuries, but are now in a stable condition. A statement released from the hospital in the early hours of this morning confirmed that Superintendent Cooper's injuries are extensive and that they may result in permanent disability. His daughter, Madeleine Cooper, sustained a bullet wound to the hip.

Jack Cooper's distinguished career in the Metropolitan Police Service began twenty-one years ago when he arrived at the Hendon Police Training College as a young graduate recruit. His recent arrest of East End businessman, Michael Stone, was only the latest of his achievements. Speculation that the assassination attempt was co-ordinated by Stone from his remand cell has been strongly denied by his lawyers. They issued a statement which said that their client had been saddened to hear of the death of Mrs Cooper, that he wished both Superintendent Cooper and his daughter a full and speedy recovery, and that a man in DCS Cooper's position must have many enemies.

Eddie Stone, Michael Stone's eldest son and acting CEO of the family's security business, Stonecor, was unavailable for comment.

Chapter One

Maddie stared out of the high window of the apartment block where she lived. It felt strange to be back home after so long in hospital. Four months. It seemed much longer. This was only her second day out in the real world. Her hip ached and she was leaning heavily on a stick. Three months of intensive physiotherapy still lay ahead of her.

She gazed blankly down at the bare trees that lined the northern boundary of Regent's Park. Beyond the barrier of leafless branches, she could make out the eccentric rooftops and enclosures of London Zoo. A fine November drizzle was falling and the whole world seemed grey and leaden and hopeless. She pushed her short blonde hair behind her ear. She'd had it cut that morning. No need to keep it long for ballet any more.

'Maddie?' Laura's voice broke into Maddie's bleak thoughts. 'Why don't you come with us to the dress rehearsal? Everyone would love to see you again.'

Maddie turned. She looked at her two friends. Laura and Sara. They were sitting on the couch. Maddie could hardly bear the anxiety and sympathy that haunted their eyes.

She smiled. 'I'd really rather not, thanks,' she said. She limped to a chair and sat, heavily and clumsily. 'I'm not very mobile at the moment.'

'That doesn't matter,' said Sara.

'Yes. It does,' Maddie said firmly. 'It matters to me.'

'But all you have to do is sit there and watch,' Laura insisted. 'It's a full dress rehearsal. You'll love it.' Her face was wrenched with pity. 'You should come. It might help.'

Maddie gave a short laugh. 'Don't worry about me,' she said. 'I'm fine.'

Sara looked closely at her. 'Are you?' she asked. 'Are you, honestly?'

'I'm doing as well as can be expected,' Maddie parroted. 'So the doctors tell me.' She gripped the stick. 'I should be able to get rid of this thing in a few weeks.' She leaned forwards, spreading her hands and attempting a smile. 'Look, I know what you're thinking, but I'm OK. Really I am.'

The door opened and Maddie's gran looked in. Jane Cooper had moved into the apartment after the shooting. 'I'm just going to the shops,' she said. 'I won't be long.'

'OK, Gran,' Maddie said, forcing a smile. 'See you later.'

'I'd be totally devastated if I found out I could never dance again,' Laura said in a low, hollow voice. She shook her head. 'I'd just die!' She put her hand to her mouth. 'Oh, Maddie. I'm so sorry. What a stupid thing to say. I'm such an idiot.'

'No, you're not,' said Maddie. 'What can you say? What can anyone say?' She took a deep breath. 'My mum's dead. My dad will probably be in a wheelchair for the rest of his life, and I'm never going to work as a professional dancer. It is awful, more awful than I can put into words, but... well, the world just carries on, doesn't it? And so must I.'

'You're so brave,' Sara murmured. 'It must be so hard without your mum.'

'As Gran keeps telling me, I've still got her in here,'

Maddie said, touching her fingertips to her forehead. She straightened her shoulders. 'Besides, Dad needs me. I have to be positive for his sake. He's working so hard at the rehabilitation unit. They say he should be home in less than two months. So the last thing he needs is for me to be wandering about feeling sorry for myself. Anyway, Mum would be really annoyed with me if I just gave up.'

'How is your dad coping?' Laura asked.

'He's pretty devastated,' Maddie admitted, 'and he's very sad and lonely without Mum, like me. But his work means a lot to him, and he's been given a new job, a really big one. Head of Police Investigation Command.'

'I've never heard of it,' Sara said. 'What do they do?'

'As far as I can tell, it's a cross between Special Branch and MI5,' Maddie told them. 'Dad reports direct to the Prime Minister. It's just perfect for him. Nothing could make Dad leave the police force now. He's going to find the man that shot us, whatever it takes.'

It seemed as if the gunman had vanished into thin air. Scotland Yard were no nearer to identifying the masked figure. Maddie knew that her father was convinced the orders had come from Michael Stone's company, Stonecor. She could only guess at how desperately he would pursue the killer with all the professional resources available to him.

'And what about you?' Laura asked, breaking into Maddie's thoughts. 'What are you going to do now?'

'I've got a few ideas,' Maddie said unconvincingly. 'Nothing definite, as yet, though. I'm still officially "sick", so I don't have to go back to school for a while. I'll think of something...'

'Anyway,' she continued, anxious to change the subject. 'You must make a move, or you'll be late, and Miss Treeves will not be amused!'

Her friends smiled and nodded.

Sara looked at her watch. 'Maddie, are you absolutely sure you won't come with us?'

'Absolutely. But thanks for thinking of me.' Maddie struggled to get to her feet. Laura reached forwards to help but a sharp glance from Maddie made her withdraw.

'I'm OK,' Maddie said. 'I can manage.' She looked steadily at her two friends. 'Now don't you dare feel sorry for me,' she said. 'And you can tell all the guys at White Lodge that I'm doing just fine. Please? Will you tell them that?'

'Of course we will,' said Laura.

Maddie walked with them, slowly, to the lift. The doors opened almost straight away. Sara walked in.

Laura turned. 'Don't lose touch,' she said.

'Of course I won't,' Maddie smiled.

Laura was clearly close to tears. 'What are you going to do, Maddie? Really?'

Maddie's eyes flashed. 'You'll see,' she said.

Laura stepped into the lift and the doors began to close.

Maddie's brave smile faded as she heard the lift going down. The sound filled her with misery. Her friends were moving away from her. Her old life was gone and there was nothing she could do to bring it back.

She limped back into the apartment, shut the door behind her and sighed. It had taken all her strength to keep up a brave face in front of her friends. She couldn't let them know how she was really feeling. How could she explain the huge black gulf ahead of her? How could they ever understand?

She went to her bedroom and sat down heavily on her bed.

She stayed like that for a few moments, gathering herself, then leaned sideways and opened the drawer of her bedside cabinet. There was a photograph inside, enclosed in a cardboard frame. She took it out.

It was of her with Mum and Dad. Taken in the dressing rooms of the Royal Opera House a few minutes after she'd come off stage that fateful Sunday night.

She gazed into her mother's face. Happy families. A million years ago in another world.

'What am I going to do, Mum?' she whispered. 'What am I going to do with the rest of my life?'

She heard a gentle but firm voice in her head. *Fate never closes one door without opening another, Maddie.*

Maddie rubbed her hand across her wet eyes. She couldn't see any open doors yet.

Her gaze moved quickly past her own beaming face. She still couldn't bear to look at herself as she had been. Some things were just too painful.

Then she looked into the loving, reliable face of her father. He still had his work – and with it, the means to stop men like her mother's killer...

Maddie's eyes widened. She looked up, blinking as if in sudden sunlight.

'Thanks, Mum,' she said softly, putting the photo back into the drawer. 'I know what I want to do now.'

Chapter Two

The long dark car glided sleekly through the streets of West London. A woman was at the wheel. She had short red hair and steady, confident, pale green eyes. Her name was Tara Moon, and she was twenty-four years old. She had been personal assistant and chauffeur to the new Detective Chief Superintendent of Police Investigation Command, Jack Cooper, for two weeks.

It was February 15th, and Tara Moon was taking her boss and his daughter to PIC Control at Centrepoint.

February 15th was also Maddie's sixteenth birthday.

In the past, her mother had always been in charge of gift-buying, so Jack Cooper had no idea what to do for his daughter. How do you celebrate when every family event just reminds you of everything you have lost?

Maddie had come up with a solution. 'If you really want to give me something special,' she had told him several days ago. 'Then I'd like a guided tour of your new department.'

Maddie had been longing to visit her father's offices. PIC Control was housed in the top four floors of Centrepoint, a curved tower of concrete and glass that soared skywards at the eastern end of Oxford Street.

Father and daughter sat back as Tara Moon navigated the big car through the heavy traffic of the Euston Road. The car had been specially adapted to take Jack Cooper's wheelchair. It also had a satellite telephone and a fax machine, and a built-in computer with email and Internet access. Maddie was impressed.

Jack Cooper looked at his daughter. 'Have you made any decisions yet, Maddie?' he asked gently. They had agreed that Maddie should use the next few months to get her life in order, and then return to her education in September. That gave her over six months to fill.

'I think so,' Maddie replied guardedly.

A wry smile flickered. 'Is it a secret?'

Maddie laughed. 'No, not especially. I just need to check a few things out first – then I'll tell you exactly what I'd like to do. OK?'

Jack Cooper nodded.

The car was moving down Gower Street now. As they turned into New Oxford Street, Maddie caught her first glimpse of Centrepoint, gleaming in the cold winter sunshine. Her heart beat fast with anticipation as she wondered what kind of place PIC Control would turn out to be. She hoped that it lived up to her expectations.

❖

The lift doors hissed open smoothly on to a scene that took Maddie's breath away.

She found herself gazing into a long, brightly lit open-plan office filled with urgent activity. Large monitor screens lined the walls, flickering with rapidly changing information. Maddie was aware of a subdued electronic hum rising from the rows of desktop servers and printers, punctuated by the soft rapid tap of keyboards. At the desk nearest to the door, a dark-haired woman wearing a lightweight headset was holding a low-voiced conversation in a language

Maddie didn't recognise. She caught Maddie's eye and grinned.

'Tara will look after you for a couple of minutes while I sort a few things out,' her father said.

Maddie looked around at him. She was feeling a little dazed.

Jack Cooper nodded at his assistant. 'Five minutes, OK?'

'Right, sir,' the assistant replied.

Tara and Maddie stepped out of the lift. The doors closed and the lift took Jack Cooper up to his private office on the top floor.

'Wow,' Maddie breathed. 'This place. It's amazing!'

Tara laughed. 'It's not always this frantic,' she said. 'All this chaos is because of the Russian President's state visit on Friday. We're on the line to make sure nothing unexpected happens.' She grinned. 'When there's something big going on out of town, this place can be almost deserted.' She touched Maddie's shoulder. 'Come on, I'll introduce you to the most important person in the entire building. Jackie Saunders, our Communications Officer.'

Maddie was led to the desk near the lift doors. Jackie Saunders sat staring at her computer screen, still speaking into her headset. She was speaking in

English now. 'I'm afraid Superintendent Cooper is not available at the moment,' she was saying. Tara waved her hand in front of the woman's face and pointed to herself.

'Oh, just a moment. I'll put you on to his PA.'

Tara picked up a phone. 'Tara Moon speaking. Can I help you?'

Maddie moved away from the desk a little and turned to watch the activity that was going on around her. She felt butterflies of excitement at the thought of being part of this confident, friendly team. Maddie wondered how her dad would react to the idea that she had been turning over in her mind.

A young man whisked past. He paused and grinned at her. He looked to be about nineteen, she guessed. Light brown hair fell over his hazel eyes. He looked fit and muscular, as if he worked out regularly.

'Is this your first day?' he asked.

'Well, yes,' Maddie said. 'I suppose so. Sort of.'

'I'm Alex,' he said.

'Maddie.'

He nodded, holding out a stiff-backed manila envelope. 'Don't worry about it, Maddie,' he said cheerfully. 'You'll soon settle in. Could you do something for me?'

'I'll try,' Maddie said.

'Thanks. Find Kevin, OK? And tell him this is the letter he's been expecting from Germany.' He grinned again and whisked off, leaving her clutching the envelope.

Maddie gazed after the good-looking young man for a few moments. She looked at the envelope and then stared around the room.

'Well, why not?' she thought.

She set off in search of Kevin.

✖

Jack Cooper pressed a button on his intercom. 'Can you tell Alex Cox to come up to my office, please,' he said. 'Right away.'

Maddie frowned at him. 'You're not going to give him a hard time, are you?' she said. 'I wouldn't have told you about it if I'd known I was getting him into trouble.' She smiled. 'Besides, it was fun.' She gave her father a thoughtful look. 'We need to talk, Dad. I've made my decision.'

'I thought you might have done.' Jack Cooper leaned back in his wheelchair. His broad black desk was cluttered with folders and files and documents. A geometric screensaver swirled across a computer monitor on a side-desk. Other tables lined the walls, laden with plain buff files. One wall was covered with a huge world map, and another with larger-scale maps of Europe and the UK. Jack Cooper's office was the nerve centre of a department whose boundaries stretched far beyond the confines of the British Isles.

At his back, a picture window offered a giddying panorama of the London skyline. Among the confusion of buildings and church spires and tower blocks, Maddie could see glimpses of the River Thames and, beyond it, the blue-hazed, leafy southern suburbs. The dome of St Paul's rose to her left; the dark Gothic filigree of the Houses of Parliament to her right. On the south bank of the river, the London Eye reared up; a great spoked wheel, its constantly moving pods glinting under the bright, winter sun.

'So, tell me what you've decided,' Maddie's father said. 'Or should I try to guess?' There was a spark of humour in his eyes.

Maddie moved around to her father's side of the desk. 'The thing is,' she began. 'I've had this idea in my head for a while now, but I wasn't sure how you'd take it. You see, what I'd really like to do, if you're OK with it, is to…' her words were broken into by a sharp knock on the door.

'Come in!' her father called.

Alex Cox stepped into the office. 'You wanted to

see me, sir?' he said. He caught sight of Maddie and smiled at her.

'Yes, Alex, I did.' Jack Cooper's deep voice rumbled across the room. 'I want to introduce you to Maddie.'

'We've already met,' Alex said brightly. He looked at Maddie. 'Did you find Kevin, OK?'

'Yes,' Maddie said. 'No problem.'

'Maddie is my daughter,' Jack Cooper growled.

Alex seemed dumbstruck for an instant, then a broad grin spread across his face. 'I suppose this rules out any chance of asking to finish early today,' he said. He gave Maddie a rueful look. 'Sorry about that stuff downstairs,' he said. 'I thought you were the new gopher.'

'I didn't mind,' Maddie said, smiling.

'My daughter is going to be doing a bit of work experience here for the next few months,' Jack Cooper said.

Maddie stared at him in astonishment. How could he possibly have known that was what she had been about to ask him?

'I want you to take her under your wing, Alex,' her father continued. 'You and Danny can show her the ropes and fill her in on how we do things around here. I'll send her down to you shortly. Make sure she's given a pass-card and knows the door codes.' He gave a curt nod. 'That's all.'

Alex turned on his heel.

'Oh, and by the way, Alex,' Jack Cooper said as the young man was pulling the door shut behind himself. 'Next time you want to off-load your work on to someone else, I suggest you check who they are first.'

'I'm way ahead of you on that one, sir,' Alex said. He shot Maddie a look of amused relief at his narrow escape and closed the door behind him. Maddie laughed, liking him immediately.

Her father looked up at her. 'Well, happy birthday, Maddie,' he said. 'I hope this is what you really want.'

She leaned over and put her arms around his neck. 'How did you know?' she asked.

'You've been interrogating me about PIC for the past month,' he said. 'It wasn't hard to figure out what was going on in your head.' He let out a rumble of laughter. 'I'm a detective, remember.'

Maddie broke the embrace and perched on the corner of his desk. 'I'm serious about this, Dad,' she said. 'I don't want to be treated differently because you're my dad. I'll do anything you say.'

'I'm glad to hear it,' he said. 'For a start you can get off my desk.'

'Oh. Sorry.' She sprang up. A twinge of pain in her hip made her grimace.

'Are you sure you're ready for this, Maddie?' her father asked. 'You could leave it for a few more weeks.'

'No way,' Maddie said firmly. 'I want to start now.' She stood erect, bringing her hand to her forehead in a mock salute. 'Where do I report, sir?'

'Go and find Alex, he'll sort you out.'

She walked to the door.

'Oh, and Maddie?'

She turned. 'Yes?'

'This isn't an endurance test,' her father said. 'You've got nothing to prove. Any problems, you come straight to me, got that?'

'Got it.'

Jack Cooper sat staring thoughtfully at the closed door for several minutes after his daughter had left the room. He wasn't certain that he was doing the right thing, but letting Maddie work here had to be better than leaving her to waste away at home.

He sighed. It was going to be tricky, but at least this way he could keep an eye on her.

The telephone rang. He picked up.

Jackie Saunders' voice sounded down the line. 'The Home Secretary for you, sir.'

Jack Cooper turned his wheelchair around to gaze out over the rooftops of London as he spoke. 'Minister, good morning,' he said. 'What can I do for you?'

'Hello, Jack,' came an authoritative female voice. 'I want to have a preliminary talk with you about the Hever Castle Economic Summit. I know it's not taking place until May, but I don't think it's too soon to start planning the security measures, and your department will be shouldering most of the responsibility.'

'One moment, Minister, while I access the file.' He spun around to face his screen.

DCS Cooper's working day had begun.

And so had Maddie's.

Chapter Three

It was a Tuesday in early May. Maddie had been working alongside Alex for twelve weeks. She was a quick learner; within days she was finding her way confidently between the various units of the complex department. She soon found that the chaos of that first day was far from relentless. As in any other office, PIC Control had days of almost unnatural calm. Like today.

'It's really weird – having the whole place to ourselves like this,' Maddie said, looking around at the deserted workstations of PIC Control. 'It's so quiet.' Apart from a few clerical staff, Alex and Maddie were virtually alone in the London headquarters. Maddie's father, and nearly everyone else, was at Hever Castle in

Kent – reinforcing the long-planned security at the economic summit.

Alex grinned at Maddie across the desk. 'Too quiet?'

She laughed. 'Yes. A bit. I like having people around me.' She leaned away from her desk and stretched. 'I wonder how Danny's getting on.' Like Alex, eighteen-year-old black American Danny Bell was a fast-track trainee in PIC.

While Alex and Maddie were holding the fort at Centrepoint, Danny was at Immigration Control at Heathrow Airport. The three of them were dealing with the Heathrow Red List of incoming passengers. This was a report of potentially undesirable visitors, produced by cross-checking the airline passenger lists against international crime investigation databanks. Ordinarily this was a fully-automated process which involved checking addresses, passport numbers and names at lightning speed. But the system had developed a fault and while the software engineers dealt with the problem, Alex and Maddie were forced to make tedious manual checks on all the incoming flights.

It wasn't unusual for Danny Bell to be out of the office; he spent most of his time on assignment, only coming into Centrepoint once or twice a week. He had been headhunted by Jack Cooper for his astonishing ability with electronics, and had designed the department's Mobile Surveillance Unit – the MSU. It looked like an ordinary Transit van but it was filled with cutting-edge surveillance technology.

Maddie liked Danny's laid-back style, even though most of their conversations so far had taken place over the phone. He made an interesting contrast to Alex's wired-up intensity.

Alex was an East End boy, born and bred. He had always wanted to join the police, from as far back as he could remember. Intelligent and quick-witted, he soon found himself on the fast-track at the Hendon Police Training College. Jack Cooper had spotting him during his first recruitment hunt, and had transferred him to PIC Control before he knew what was happening.

Maddie sank her chin into her fists as she watched Alex scrolling down the Red List for the fifth consecutive hour. 'I wonder what's happening at the summit?' she said. 'Do you think there'll be any problems?'

'I doubt it,' Alex said. 'I think they've got it pretty much under wraps.'

'I bet you wish you were over there,' she said.

He smiled wryly. 'Don't you?'

41

'Well, it's got to be an improvement on this,' she said, waving a hand towards Alex's computer. 'This is so dull.'

'It has to be done,' Alex said with a wry smile. 'Let's hope the fault is sorted out by tomorrow.' He laughed. 'You enjoy most of the work, though, don't you?'

Maddie smiled. 'Of course I do,' she said. 'Most of it. But I can't get very excited about checking endless flight lists on the off-chance of spotting someone interesting. We've been doing it all day. I'm starting to see double.' She looked at the clock. 'It's five-fifteen,' she said. 'We can quit soon, can't we? No one will know if we skive off a few minutes early.'

'OK,' Alex said. 'Ten more minutes, then we're out of here.'

'Slave-driver!' Maddie said. She knew Alex didn't enjoy this kind of routine work any more than she did. But he was dogged and persistent, she'd learned that much about him. Give him a job, and he'd see it through to the end no matter what.

'Do you fancy a snack after work?' Maddie asked. 'My treat.' Her gran was out of town for a few days, and it struck Maddie that she didn't have much reason to rush home.

'Later, maybe,' Alex said. 'I'm going to need an

hour or so in the gym to loosen up after this.' He glanced at her. One of the perks of the job was the fully-equipped gym in the basement. Alex often used the place to work off excess energy – especially after a chairbound day like today. 'Do you fancy a workout?' he asked her. Then he frowned. 'Oh. Sorry. Your hip. I forgot.'

It had been ten months since Maddie had done any exercise beyond the physiotherapy prescribed by her doctors and she missed the adrenaline rush of physical activity.

'I think it's about time I forgot about it, too,' she said. Her eyes shone. 'I can't spend the rest of my life being careful.'

'OK,' Alex said. 'The gym opens at half five. That gives us time to check a few more flight lists before we knock off.'

'Great,' Maddie sighed. 'So. Where were we?'

'Afternoon flights from Boston, USA,' Alex said. 'Ready?'

Maddie clicked to bring up the Red List on her screen. 'Go ahead,' she said.

'OK. Flight AA101. Scheduled to arrive at Terminal 3 at 17:45, our time.'

Alex pressed out instructions on his keyboard and hit the ENTER key.

Maddie watched the flickering blur of names. Her screen came to a halt.

'I've got a positive on someone called Grace O'Connor,' she told Alex. She manoeuvred the mouse. 'Let's see what she's done wrong, then. Want to make a guess?'

'International arms smuggling,' suggested Alex.

'I'll go for illegal parking,' Maddie laughed. Her screen filled with a new file. The American crest in the top left hand corner showed this was a download from FBI files. There was a list of information and a full-length photograph.

Grace O'Connor was twenty years old. Her startlingly attractive face was framed by short blonde hair. Maddie's eyes widened. She was sure that she'd seen the dress Grace was wearing in *Vogue* – in a feature on Prada. The angle of her head and the look in her blue eyes gave an impression of cool disdain, as if she was a person used to getting her own way.

Maddie double clicked the mouse and read out the information that appeared. 'Here it is,' she said. 'She was picked up at Boston's Logan Airport on two separate occasions in the past two years with a small amount of cocaine in her luggage. Neither case came to court.'

Alex leaned across to look at her screen. 'Is that so?' he said. 'I wonder why?'

'Hmm... it doesn't say.'

The file showed that her father's name was Patrick Fitzgerald O'Connor. There was a red dot beside his name. 'What does that mean?' Maddie asked, pointing at the dot.

'It means her dad is on the Red List as well,' Alex said. 'Interesting. Open it up, and let's see why.'

Maddie did so, and a new file opened.

The photo was of a distinguished man in a business suit. He had dark, deep-set eyes, and the stern, steady gaze of a powerful man.

Maddie began to read aloud. 'Patrick Fizgerald O'Connor. Boston businessman. Known as 'Teflon Pat'. Wealthy and influential. Heads twenty-one corporations throughout America. It is known that O'Connor's business empire was built on money gained some years ago in suspicious circumstances, but nothing has been found that could be used against him. All his businesses appear to be legitimate and he likes to be seen as a pillar of the community with hefty donations to various charities. Long-term FBI investigation is under way to assess any potential for a court case on tax avoidance.'

'So,' Maddie said, 'reading between the lines, they think he's a crook, but they can't prove it, yes?'

'It looks that way,' Alex said.

'And the girl flying into Heathrow this evening is his daughter?'

'If it is her, that would explain how she got away with the two drugs busts,' Alex said. 'Daddy must have pulled some strings for her.' He tapped at the keyboard. 'I'll just run a quick trace to confirm that the Grace O'Connor on our file is the same as the one on the aeroplane. With any luck, the tickets will have been paid for by credit card.' He logged on to another site and the screen changed rapidly.

'That's it,' he said. 'Tickets paid for by American Express platinum card in the name of Grace O'Connor of Commonwealth Avenue, Boston. That's her, OK!'

'So, what do we do now?' Maddie asked.

Alex switched his PC into telephone mode and keyed a mobile phone number. He grinned at Maddie. 'We have a quick word with Danny. He stops her at Customs and very carefully checks her luggage. If she's carrying any suspicious little parcels, she'll be in big trouble. Let's see her daddy try to get her out of that!'

Chapter four

Terminal Three, Heathrow Airport was buzzing. Danny Bell walked quickly through the shopping area, back towards the Arrivals Zone. He had finished his shift at Passport Control and had been out on the rooftop terrace, chilling out and watching the planes, when the call had come through from Alex.

Danny tapped urgently into his mobile as he cut his way through the milling crowds. A computer file scrolled up on the little screen. The picture of Grace O'Connor began to reveal itself.

Danny raised an eyebrow as he looked at the glamorous young woman. Definitely a Gucci-babe. Money gleamed behind those blue eyes. Rich kid gone bad. Caught twice with drugs in her luggage. Not a lady to learn from her mistakes, then. Still, why worry, when Daddy's there to bail you out?

Danny read her father's file. His eyes narrowed. O'Connor might appear to be squeaky-clean these days, but his fortune was based on criminal money. Danny knew the type. Mobsters in Armani suits: sober on the outside and pure poison underneath.

Danny had good reason to know about people like Patrick O'Connor. People like him were the reason why Danny and his father had come to London in the first place.

During a quiet moment at the coffee machine a few weeks ago, Danny had told Maddie that Bell wasn't his real name, and that he and his father were in London under the FBI Witness Relocation Scheme. They were on the run from the Chicago Mob after his father had given evidence against them in a big trial.

'If they tracked us down,' Danny ran a finger across his throat as he spoke, 'we'd be lying in the foundations of some new road system within twenty-four hours!'

She had stared at him in shock. 'You will be, if you go around telling everyone,' she had said.

He had looked carefully at her. 'I trust you,' he had said simply. 'You, and Alex... I'm right to trust you, aren't I?'

'Yes,' Maddie had said. 'Yes, of course.'

Danny smiled to himself at the memory of that conversation. He still wasn't sure why he had confided in Maddie like that – there was just something about her. Not that he had told her the whole truth. Oh no. Not quite. The whole truth was a secret between Danny and his father, and there was no way anyone else was ever going to find that out.

Danny's eyes focused again on the face of Grace O'Connor as she gazed coolly out from the screen of his mobile. Her plane would be touching down in a quarter of an hour. And Danny would be waiting for her.

✖

Danny stood near the entrance to Customs. He spotted Grace O'Connor almost instantly. She wasn't the kind of person you'd miss in a crowd. Attractive, blonde, wearing a simple black dress, probably Prada, carrying the tiniest little Louis Vuitton handbag...

He wondered who her companion was. Boyfriend, obviously. She was clinging tightly on to his arm, gazing into his face like she was afraid he might vanish if she blinked. Sharp dresser. The son of someone big in Boston, maybe.

Danny watched as the couple made their way

through the crowd towards Baggage Reclaim. The man stepped forward and swung a couple of small suitcases off the carousel. Grace and her boyfriend were travelling light.

Danny slipped back into the Customs area as they headed towards him. He waited unobtrusively, leaning against the wall. Watching. Grace and boyfriend walked towards the Green Exit. Nothing To Declare.

Yeah, right! thought Danny.

He slid quietly past them and came up alongside the Customs Officer on duty by the exit. He flashed his PIC card as he spoke to the uniformed woman, 'I'll handle the approaching couple, if that's OK.'

The Customs Officer looked at Danny. Her eyes widened briefly, then she nodded and stood aside.

The couple were walking separately now, but close together. The man was carrying both suitcases. Grace was squeezing the life out of her handbag. She looked nervous. Jumpy even.

Danny stepped forward. He smiled as he held a hand up to stop them. 'Excuse me,' he said politely. 'May I ask you to step over here for a moment, please.'

'Sure,' the man said. His voice was tense but controlled. 'What can we do for you?'

'It's just routine,' Danny said, ushering the couple

over to a low desk where the Customs Officer was waiting. She handed him a clipboard. 'Could you read this form, please,' she said, 'and tell me if are carrying any of the items that are on the list?'

Grace now had hold of her handbag with both hands, clutching it against her stomach. Her face had gone white. There was a hint of barely-controlled panic behind her eyes.

The man looked at the form. 'No, I don't believe we are,' he said. He smiled coldly at Danny as he handed the form back. 'Is that all?'

Danny looked at Grace. 'Did you pack these bags yourselves?' he asked.

'Yes.' Grace's voice was a low croak. She coughed. 'Yes, we did.' She pointed from bag to bag. 'That one's mine – and that one's Henry's. They just contain clothes and toiletries and stuff.'

Danny nodded. He made a casual gesture towards the handbag. 'And would you like to tell me what's in there, please?'

Grace opened her mouth to speak, but her companion cut her off. 'You know the kind of stuff,' he said. 'Make-up and a few pieces of jewellery.' He smiled ingratiatingly. 'All the usual junk girls have to carry around with them.'

Danny nodded again. 'I'd like to take a quick look inside, if that's OK with you, miss,' he said.

Henry's voice wavered for the first time. 'And if it isn't?'

Danny stared coolly into his eyes. 'I'd like to take a quick look, anyhow,' he said. 'It'll only take a moment.' He looked at Grace. 'Could you place your bag on the desk and open it for me, please?'

More than ever, Danny was now convinced that he was going to find something interesting in that handbag.

Grace seemed paralysed, clinging on to the bag as though her life depended on it.

Henry looked sharply at her. 'You'd better do it,' he muttered. 'Get it over with.'

She shot him a scared look.

Oh, yes! thought Danny. *We've got something here, all right.*

Grace placed the handbag on the desk. She fumbled for a few moments with the catch. Her fingers were shaking almost too much for her to be able to get it open. 'I'm sorry,' she murmured.

'Take your time,' Danny said smoothly.

She finally got the catch loose. Danny took hold of the handbag and drew it across the desk.

Henry hadn't been lying. There was a lot of La Prairie make-up in there. And there were some small boxes that obviously contained jewellery. Danny pulled one box out and opened it. A solid gold bracelet gleamed against maroon velvet. He raised his eyebrows but remained silent, clipping the box shut and putting it back.

Danny sifted carefully through the rest of the contents. Quietly and methodically, he emptied the handbag, placing every item on the desk. He felt the lining, searching for anything hidden underneath. He ran his fingertips along the bottom of the bag and found a small tear. Pulling it open, he saw a small pouch made of dark blue felt. He drew it out.

'What's in here?' he asked Grace.

She began to speak, but again, Henry cut her off. 'A few fake stones,' he said glibly. 'Fake diamonds. You know? Paste. We promised Grace's little sister we'd have a necklace made for her while we were in London. In Hatton Garden – you know – the diamond place. We're going to have them make her a nice-looking necklace. The stones are only worth a few dollars.'

Danny looked at him coolly. 'You're going to get a specialist diamond merchant in Hatton Garden to make a necklace from imitation diamonds?' he said.

'And you ripped up the lining of a Louis Vuitton handbag to make sure these worthless diamonds were hidden safely away?' He stared at them. 'That's an odd thing to do...'

He loosened the drawstrings of the pouch. 'May I?' he said.

'They're fakes, I can assure you,' Henry said, laughing uneasily.

Danny opened his hand and poured the contents of the pouch into his palm. The other Customs Officer leaned close. There had to be thirty or more gemstones there, all of them two carats or more, sparkling like flashlights.

The officer whispered in Danny's ear. 'They're real.'

Danny nodded. This wasn't at all what he had been expecting; instead of an illicit stash of cocaine, he was now holding a small fortune in smuggled diamonds in the palm of his hand.

'They belong to Grace,' Henry said, trying to sound like he had some control over the situation. 'They're hers. There's no question about it. You have no reason to prevent us from continuing with our journey. We have to meet with someone. It's important. He's expecting us.'

'Sorry, but he'll have to wait,' Danny said. He lifted

his eyes to look right into Grace's pale face. 'I don't believe that these are fakes, miss. I think they're real. In which case you have some serious explaining to do.'

Chapter Five

Maddie and Alex had abandoned all thought of leaving the office. If there was any chance of Danny finding illegal substances in Grace O'Connor's luggage, they wanted to be on the spot when he reported back.

It was 18:33. The plane from Boston had landed nearly an hour ago. Alex couldn't keep still. He was walking up and down behind his workstation, restless and impatient.

Maddie was sitting at her PC, staring at the picture of Grace O'Connor on the screen as she waited for Danny's call.

'What's he doing over there?' Alex said. 'The plane

landed on time. It shouldn't be taking this long.'

'Some hold-up at Baggage Reclaim, maybe?' Maddie said. 'Should I give him a call?'

'No. He might be with her. We should wait for him to contact us.' Alex looked at his watch. 'We'll give him till six forty-five.'

Suddenly the telephone rang shrilly.

Maddie dived for the headset. 'Yes?'

'You're not going to believe what I'm holding in my hand right now,' came Danny's voice. 'Here's a clue: it begins with a D, but it isn't Drugs.'

Alex quickly picked up a second headset. 'What have you got for us, Danny?'

'Diamonds,' Danny replied. 'I found a whole fistful of diamonds in the lining of her handbag. Grace and her boyfriend said they were fake, but they're the definite article. Must be worth millions of pounds.'

Alex frowned. 'Do you think Patrick O'Connor is in on this?'

'I think it's likely,' Danny replied. 'Grace's boyfriend – guy named Henry Dean – says he works for her father. They're in separate interview rooms now and I'm just about to go and talk to them. Thought you'd want to know the score so far.' He laughed. 'This looks like it could be real big league stuff, guys.'

'Report back as soon as you can,' Alex said.

'Sure thing.' The line went silent as Danny hung up. Alex and Maddie looked at one another.

'So we might really be on to something here?' Maddie asked, eyes gleaming.

Alex nodded. He turned to the keyboard. 'Let's see if we can get any background on Mr Dean.'

✪

Henry Dean was perspiring heavily under his Brooks Brothers suit. Thin rivulets ran down his face. He sat opposite Danny, tapping his fingertips restlessly on the table. 'This is harassment,' he blustered. 'Miss O'Connor and I have done nothing wrong.' His eyes flashed. 'We've come to England as tourists. For a vacation. We don't expect to be treated this way.'

Danny rested back in his chair, leaning a notepad against the edge of the desk. He was watching Henry Dean, trying to figure him out. 'The diamonds are real, sir,' he said. 'Why did you lie to me about them? That makes me very suspicious.'

'I did not lie,' Dean said very slowly. 'To the best of my knowledge, the diamonds that Miss O'Connor was carrying were imitation. Neither of us had any reason to believe otherwise.'

'I see.' Employing interrogation skills taught to him

by Jack Cooper, Danny pursed his lips thoughtfully, letting his prey sweat a little more. He scribbled a few words on his notepad.

You are so lying, buddy!

After a lengthy pause, Danny asked, 'So, if the diamonds are fakes, Mr Dean, why were they hidden in the bottom of Miss O'Connor's bag?'

Dean's fingers stopped tapping. 'I have no idea,' he snapped. 'You should be asking Miss O'Connor that, not me – it's her bag!'

Danny smiled. 'Oh, don't worry, sir,' he replied. 'I'll certainly be asking her the same question.' Then he waited a little longer before asking, 'By the way, Mr Dean, just what is your relationship with Miss O'Connor?'

Dean cleared his throat. 'She is my employer's daughter,' he said. 'I was asked by Mr O'Connor to accompany her on her trip to London. He doesn't like her to travel alone. I'm sure you can understand why.'

'So, you're her chaperone?' Danny asked.

Dean nodded.

'Nothing else?' Danny persisted.

'Of course not,' he snapped. 'What are you getting at?'

'The two of you were holding hands when I

intercepted you,' Danny said. 'And the way she was looking at you – well, if I were her father, I wouldn't want her looking at an employee of mine like that.' Danny looked Dean right in the eye. 'I might get kind of suspicious that something was going on behind my back if I was her father – know what I mean?'

'I have no more to say,' Dean declared tightly. 'Except that I object to your line of questioning. I'd like to see your superior.'

'That might be a bit tricky,' Danny said. 'He's in Kent right now.' Danny's mobile chimed. He slid it out of his pocket. The call was from Control. It was Alex.

'We've been checking on your Mr Dean,' Alex said. 'He's on O'Connor's payroll. He's an accountant. Nothing special. No criminal record. But Maddie's found something interesting. I'll hand you over.'

Maddie came on to the line. 'Hi, Danny. I did a check on their flight tickets. They both have one-way tickets to London, bought on Grace's credit card, but here's the killer – Henry's got a separate ticket that was bought on a later date, using his own card. A one-way ticket on Swissair to Zurich. He's only on a twenty-four hour stopover in London.'

'Interesting,' said Danny. 'Leave it with me. I'll get back to you.'

Danny put his mobile away. He smiled at Dean. 'So, tell me,' he said. 'Who's going to be looking after Grace while you're in Switzerland?'

✖

Danny was in the corridor between the two interview rooms, speaking to Control on his mobile. 'As soon as I mentioned Switzerland, Dean just clammed up,' he said. 'He won't say a word now. But there's something really screwy going on here.'

'I know what you're thinking,' Alex said. 'Why hasn't he asked for a phone? If he was here under Patrick O'Connor's orders, you'd expect him to scream for help the moment he was picked up.'

'That's right,' said Danny. 'If I was him, I'd be asking for a lawyer. Either that, or I'd want someone from the American Embassy brought down here. But the guy is just sitting there, sweating it out and saying nothing. I don't get it.'

'What do you think is going on, guys?' Maddie asked. 'Is O'Connor using his daughter and this accountant guy to courier diamonds into the country illegally, or what?'

'I don't think so,' said Alex. 'That doesn't explain the one-way tickets. If they were only here to hand over some hot diamonds, they'd want to fly back to

America some time soon. And even if they were planning on taking an extended holiday over here, surely they'd have bought open-ended return tickets.'

'Good point,' said Maddie. 'The only reason for buying one-way tickets is if you don't plan on going back for a long time. Or at all.'

'Have you spoken to Grace yet?' Alex asked.

'I'm on my way,' said Danny. 'Maybe she'll be more willing to talk when I tell her about her boyfriend's single ticket to sample the Swiss fresh air.'

✪

From her puffy red eyes, it was obvious that Grace O'Connor had been crying. Danny brought her a cup of coffee, but she ignored it. She'd been sitting in the bare white interview room for more than thirty minutes. Plenty of time to think – and to start feeling really sorry for herself.

But Grace seemed to have got over her tears now, as she sat, ashen-faced across from Danny. Her back was ramrod straight and there was defiance in her eyes.

'I want to see Henry,' she said. 'We've done nothing wrong. Those diamonds belong to me. I hid them in the lining of my bag because I was worried that if someone saw the pouch I might be robbed. I'm sure that even you can understand that. All this nonsense has gone on long enough. I want to see Henry, and I want you to stop all this and let us go.'

'Have some coffee,' Danny said. 'It's OK. By British standards.'

'I don't want coffee,' Grace said. 'I want you to let me go.'

'Go where?' Danny asked.

She frowned. 'Excuse me?'

'It's a simple enough question,' said Danny. 'If I released you, where would you go?'

'I don't see how that's any of your business,' Grace said coldly.

'Skiing, maybe?' Danny said. 'Mountain climbing?'

The young woman frowned at him. 'What are you talking about?'

'I'm talking about Switzerland. Oh, of course...' Danny clicked his fingers. 'I forgot – you're not going to Switzerland, are you? Mr Dean is going on his own.'

It took a few seconds for this to register. 'Don't be absurd. Henry and I are staying in London.'

Danny shook his head. 'I'm afraid not, Miss O'Connor. Your boyfriend has a one-way ticket to Zurich. Didn't you know? Didn't he mention it?' Danny leaned forward, not giving her time to recover. 'Now, why don't you tell me the truth about those diamonds?' He slipped his PIC identity card out of his wallet and pushed it across the desk to her. 'I'm a police officer, Miss O'Connor.'

Her eyes widened in shock, then narrowed. 'You can't be,' she said. 'You're not old enough.'

'I'm old enough to fix you up with a night in a cell,' Danny said. 'Either we do this here, or I have you taken to a police station. It's your choice.'

There was a silence while Grace O'Connor took this in. 'You're American,' she said. 'Are you with the FBI?'

'No, I'm with the British police, and I'm getting tired of you lying to me, Grace,' Danny replied. 'Now, are you going to tell me about those diamonds or are we going to sit here all night?'

The defiance in Grace O'Connor's eyes began to crumble. Her mouth trembled. 'But if Henry's got a ticket to Zurich...' she began.

Danny waited.

Her hands came up to cover her face. 'What have I done?' she mumbled. 'I've been so stupid!'

Danny sat silently, giving her a few minutes to pull herself together. There were fresh tears on her face when she raised her head to look at him.

'My father doesn't approve of me and Henry,'

Grace began. 'He refused to let us marry. We were running away together.'

Danny was impressed by the firmness in her voice, given the circumstances.

'It was Henry's idea,' she went on. 'He planned the whole thing. He had me take the diamonds from my father's safe at home. My father is out of town for a few days, so we knew we'd have time to get far away before anyone found they'd gone missing.'

'You bought the tickets with your credit card,' Danny said. 'That was pretty dumb, wasn't it? How long do you think it would have taken your father to track you down?'

More tears fell silently down Grace's cheeks. 'Henry told me to pay with cash, but I forgot to draw it out in time – and I didn't want him getting mad with me. So I used the card...' She looked into Danny's face. 'Henry was planning to leave without me, wasn't he? He was going to take the money and run. He never wanted me – he just wanted the diamonds.'

'It looks that way,' Danny answered softly.

Grace O'Connor's eyes glittered angrily. 'Well, he won't get them now. I won't lift a finger to help him out of this.'

Danny watched her. 'So,' he said, 'you cracked your

father's safe – you bought two tickets to London – what was the plan after that?'

'We were meant to meet up with a man at the airport,' Grace said. 'Henry knew about him – I don't know how. The man was going to give us cash in exchange for the diamonds. Henry said we needed to get rid of the diamonds as quickly as possible.'

'So, is this guy waiting for you now? Here?'

'I guess so,' Grace said. 'It doesn't matter any more. Nothing matters. I just want to go home!'

Danny thought she was about to lose her composure again, but she pulled herself together, too proud to be seen crying.

'Do you know the name of this man you were supposed to meet?' he persisted.

Grace took a few deep breaths. 'Bryson, I think...' she said. 'Yes, Richard Bryson.'

Danny stood up. 'Thank you, Miss O'Connor!' He was already pulling his mobile out as he left the room. Alex and Maddie would want to hear this. If Richard Bryson was a big enough fish to fence millions of dollars' worth of diamonds in one hit, then he was someone that PIC needed to know about – if they didn't already have him in their sights.

❶

'Richard Bryson?' Maddie said, looking at Alex. 'Mean anything to you?'

Alex shook his head. 'I'll run him through the files.'

Maddie still had Grace's picture up on her screen. She spoke to Danny through the headset. 'Does she look as good in real life as she does in the photo?'

'No...' came Danny's reply. 'Better.'

'So? What's the deal?' Maddie asked. 'Is she madly in love with Henry Dean, or what?'

'She probably thought she was,' Danny replied. 'But she went off him real quick when she found out about Zurich.'

Alex let out a low whistle as he stared at his computer screen.

'Hold on, Danny,' Maddie said. She looked at Alex. 'I think we have a file.'

'We do indeed,' Alex said. 'Are you listening to this, Danny?'

'Sure am.'

'Richard Bryson is on Stonecor's board of directors.'

Maddie felt as if she'd been punched in the stomach. 'Stonecor...' she murmured. 'That means Richard Bryson works for Michael Stone.' The horror of that rainy night came flooding back.

Alex felt a rush of sympathy as he realised why she

looked so pale. 'There's more,' he said. 'Bryson is Stonecor's Deputy Chairman. He is – he was – Michael Stone's right-hand man.'

Chapter Six

Danny heard this too, and whistled softly.

Alex continued to read from the file on Richard Bryson. 'According to this, he took part in all of Stone's major decisions.'

'Anyone that close to Stone has to be hip-deep in the bad stuff,' Danny said. 'Do we have anything on him?'

'No,' Alex replied. 'He's clean. Whiter than white. Just like the rest of Stonecor. Untouchable.'

'Not any more, he isn't,' said Maddie shortly. 'Not if he's at Heathrow with a bag full of money – waiting to do a trade on a pile of stolen diamonds. That's fencing.'

'It would have been,' Danny's voice broke in, 'if we hadn't wrecked the whole deal by picking Grace and boyfriend up before they could get to him.'

'If we could get to Bryson,' Alex said, 'it might be an opening right into the middle of Stonecor, now Michael Stone is no longer there to guard his empire. Maybe Eddie Stone isn't so careful...'

'It's too late,' Danny said. 'The deal's blown.'

'It could still work,' Alex said to Danny. 'Could you bargain with Grace? Get her to follow it through? Meet with Bryson like they'd arranged?'

'No way,' Danny said. 'She's a wreck. She'd never hold it together. All she wants to do is get the diamonds back to Daddy and pretend this whole thing never happened.'

Maddie stared at the picture of Grace O'Connor. The germ of an idea was beginning to form in her mind. 'Danny,' she asked. 'Has she ever met Bryson before?'

'No. She told me Henry always dealt with him.'

Slowly Maddie leaned forward. 'Danny, can you find out whether Bryson actually knows what Grace and Henry look like?' she asked.

'Sure thing,' Danny said. 'I'll be back.' The line was cut.

Alex was looking at Maddie. 'What's the plan?' he asked.

'Give me a second.' Maddie cruised her mouse over its pad. When she'd finished, pictures of Grace O'Connor and Henry Dean lay side by side on her screen. 'Do you think I could pass for twenty?' she asked Alex.

Alex stared at Maddie. 'I'd say so,' he said. 'Why?'

Maddie shook her head impatiently. 'Are you any good at accents?' she asked.

'I was pretty cool in our school production of *Grease*!' Alex said with a half-smile.

'I'm not bad, either,' Maddie grinned. 'One of my best friends comes from Philadelphia.' She slipped easily into an American accent. 'Her name was Jacqueline Hulton. I used to do impersonations of her. The guys all thought it was so neat.'

'Hidden talents,' Alex said, grinning back. His own voice took on an American drawl: 'I was real keen on acting as a kid,' he said. 'I kind of wanted to go on the stage, but my parents, like, totally disapproved. They said I should get myself a nice, safe, steady job.'

Maddie's eyes gleamed. 'We could do it, Alex. We could be Grace and Henry. We could meet up with Bryson.'

Alex nodded wildly as he thought it through. 'The moment he does the change-over – the diamonds for the cash – we call in Airport Security,' he said.

'And when the boss gets home from the Economic Summit,' Maddie said, her eyes shining, 'we'll have one of Stonecor's top executives locked up on charges of receiving stolen goods!'

✖

The call from Heathrow came through a few minutes later.

'Guys?' Danny's voice crackled.

'Hi, Danny!' Maddie called. 'So, have Bryson and Henry ever met?'

'No,' Danny replied. 'They've exchanged a few e-mails, but that's all.'

'They've been talking about stuff like this on e-mail?' Maddie said. 'Isn't that dangerous for them?'

'Stonecor is a security business, Maddie,' Alex reminded her. 'They've installed an impassable firewall. PIC have been trying to hack into it for ages but Stonecor are always one step ahead of us.'

Danny's line crackled through again. 'I'll say one thing for our Mr Dean, guys,' he said. 'He knows when to quit: folded like a pocket handkerchief when I mentioned Richard Bryson; told me the whole deal.

And – trust me – you're not going to believe this.' Danny paused. 'According to Henry, Patrick O'Connor and our very own Michael Stone had been holding secret talks about a transatlantic business deal. They were talking right up to the time Stone was arrested. Eddie Stone has taken over the negotiations now. Their representatives have been working on a deal for months. Apparently there are some problems and the talks are at a critical stage.'

'So, Henry got to know about Bryson's "fencing activities" via the Stonecor/O'Connor deal?' Alex deduced.

'That's right.' There was a hint of excitement even in Danny's usually impassive voice. 'This is heavy stuff, guys. If we can reel Bryson in and get him to talk, we might be able to bust this whole thing wide open – on both sides of the Atlantic. But where do we go from here?'

'Maddie has a plan,' Alex said.

'Danny,' Maddie said. 'Alex and I are going to impersonate Grace and Henry.'

'Say that again?'

'It could work, Danny,' Maddie insisted. 'Alex and I are going to get over to Heathrow as quickly as possible.'

'And meanwhile, Danny,' Alex added, 'you need to get out to the Arrivals area and page Richard Bryson. It's been a while now since the plane landed, but I'm betting he'll still be there. There's too much money involved for him to have just given up already. Page him and tell him that Grace and Henry have been delayed.'

'Delayed by what?' came Danny's voice.

'You'll think of something, Danny,' Maddie said. 'Just stall him. Hold him there till we arrive. And Danny – have you got the diamonds?'

'Sure, but—'

'Good,' said Alex. 'Hold on to them for us. We're going to need them if we're going to pull this off.'

'Wait a minute—'

'See you soon, Danny,' Maddie said. She cut contact.

'We don't have long, Maddie,' warned Alex. 'There's only one way we can get there fast enough – I just hope you have the stomach for it!'

Chapter Seven

A silver Ducati came surging up from the deep basement of Centrepoint. The sky above London was already dark, and traffic was heavy.

Maddie clung on to the back of the motorbike as Alex threaded his way westwards. They sped along Piccadilly and around Hyde Park Corner. Two more rapid shifts of direction, and they were hurtling past Hammersmith towards the M4 and Heathrow Airport.

The fierce wind lashed at Maddie's face. She felt exhilarated. It still astounded her – the way events had snowballed. A few hours ago, all they had was a name on a computer file. Now, they were taking on top-level operators from criminal empires on both sides of the Atlantic.

Meanwhile, all Danny had to do was to keep Richard Bryson on site until they arrived. And if Alex kept this speed up, that wasn't going to take too long!

✪

Danny was at the American Airlines information desk. Richard Bryson had been paged, and now all he could do was to wait and hope that the Stonecor executive would respond.

'Excuse me, my name is Richard Bryson. I believe I'm wanted?'

The sharply dressed man was in his thirties. His black hair was cropped short above his angular, close-shaven face. He was carrying a Zero Halliburton attaché case.

Danny did his best to seem casual, as if there was nothing unusual going on, but his heart was pounding. 'Ah, yes, that's right,' he said, smiling professionally. He flicked through some papers, faking a search. 'Here we are. It's a message from a Mr Dean,' he said casually, glancing up to assess the effect of the name.

Richard Bryson's face didn't show a thing.

'Mr Dean has asked us to let you know that Miss O'Connor was taken ill on the plane, and that she's currently waiting to see a doctor.'

Richard Bryson leaned over the high desk, frowning slightly. 'Is it anything serious?'

'No. Not at all. She was just a little flight-sick,' Danny said. 'But she's asked to see a doctor. Mr Dean has said that he and Miss O'Connor will be with you in as short a time as possible.'

Richard Bryson slid back the cuff of his shirt and looked at his Rolex watch, shaking his head. 'Will you have me paged?'

'Of course, sir,' Danny replied politely.

As Bryson moved away from the information desk, he drew a mobile phone from his pocket and tapped out a number.

✖

Alex and Maddie ran along the main concourse of Terminal Three. The journey to Heathrow had been a wild, breathtaking ride, with Alex leaning heavily on the throttle every chance he got.

'Have you got a credit card on you?' Maddie asked.

'Of course,' Alex replied.

'Good.' Maddie raced up to an information board. 'There's nothing suitable here – we'll have to go airside.' She grabbed Alex's arm and pulled him towards the entrance to the Departure lounges. Feeling rather bemused, Alex watched as Maddie talked urgently to a uniformed official and flashed her PIC pass. Moments later, the official hurried them through a side door into the brightly lit airside shopping area. Maddie made straight for the discreet maroon-painted Ferragamo outlet.

'I'll be as quick as I can!' she called.

Following her, Alex reached for his wallet. 'Maddie, I'm not sure my credit limit will stretch to this place. Don't go crazy!' he called back.

Maddie grinned, grabbed two dresses from a nearby rail and hurried into the changing room.

◉

Danny sat in one of the interview rooms. He was tipping the diamonds from hand to hand. Watching them sparkle. The female customs officer sat nearby. Grace and Henry's luggage lay on the table between them.

From within Henry Dean's jacket, the mobile began to ring.

'That's gotta be about the tenth call Bryson has made to Henry,' Danny said. 'I think he's getting impatient.' He looked at his watch: 20:34.

The phone cut off.

Then a different tone sounded – this time from Danny's pocket. He took out his mobile.

'It's Alex,' came the familiar voice.

'Where are you?' Danny asked. 'If you don't get here soon, Richard Bryson's gonna skip.'

'We're already here,' Alex said.

'Where?'

'Just crossing the check-in hall,' came the voice. 'We'll be with you in five, OK?'

✪

Danny's eyes opened wide as Maddie swept in dressed in a stunning black Ferragamo dress and elegant high-heeled shoes.

Maddie had never been in and out of a clothes shop so quickly in her life. She was thankful that the Departures official had been so helpful. But she had chosen well, and looked good. She sat at the table in the interview room and, using a small mirror, began to apply La Prairie make-up borrowed from Grace O'Connor's handbag.

'How much did it cost?' Danny asked.

'Don't ask,' Alex said.

Danny smiled. 'That much?'

Alex nodded. 'I hope that I can claim it on expenses.'

'I'm sure you can,' Maddie said. Then she grinned. 'Probably,' she added.

Alex rolled his eyes at Danny, he'd smartened up with a new jacket and a designer shirt for half the price of Maddie's outfit.

Then Maddie laid down the lipstick and turned to face them. 'Well?' she said. 'Will I do?'

Danny and Alex looked at her and both nodded approvingly.

'You've convinced me,' Alex said with a smile.

'What's happening to the real Grace and Henry,' asked Maddie.

'Oh customs will keep them busy for the next few hours, don't worry,' said Danny. 'OK, guys,' he continued. 'I've brought a few little gizmos over from the tracker van – just in case things don't go completely according to plan.' He had two short strips of black tape in his palm. 'These are tracers,' he said. 'You peel the back off to activate them. You can attach 'em to just about anything. Once they've been activated, they'll run for around twelve hours, and they put out a signal that I can pick up in the MSU from up to 200 metres away.' Danny peeled the backing tape off one of the tracers and carefully stuck it to the inside of the pouch that held the diamonds.

He handed the second tracer to Maddie. 'Put that

somewhere discreet,' he advised. Maddie peeled the backing tape off and placed it just inside the hem of her dress.

'Good,' Danny said. 'Now we won't lose you or the diamonds.' He turned to Alex. 'I'm going to wire you up,' he said. He produced a wireless electronic earpiece no bigger than a thumb-tack and a tiny, flat transmitter. A lightweight throat-mike fastened to the top button of Alex's shirt with a hair-thin wire loop.

The transmitter was taped to Alex's chest under his shirt. The earpiece fitted neatly and unobtrusively.

Alex re-adjusted his clothes.

'Perfect,' said Danny. 'Unless someone decides to give you a pretty thorough shakedown, there's no way they'll know you're carrying.'

'How close do you have to be for us to talk?' Alex asked.

'My mobile's been adapted to transmit and receive up to about ten metres,' Danny said. 'But I've got booster-gear in the van that means I can be 200 metres away and still hear you clearly. Oh, and Alex,' Danny added, 'that earpiece is a prototype, so don't lose it, or Cooper will kill the whole bunch of us.'

Maddie stood up, smoothing down her dress. Her palms were damp and her heart thudding. She looked at Danny and Alex and saw their anxious eyes on her. Could she really pull this off?

She had to.

She took a few deep breaths to calm herself, then said, 'This is it, then, guys...'

Alex and Danny nodded.

The diamonds went back into the handbag. Maddie picked it up. She reached for one of the suitcases.

'No,' Danny said. 'Grace would never carry her own bags.'

Alex took both suitcases. 'Let's go,' he said.

They walked along the corridor towards the main Arrivals area.

'OK,' Alex said. 'We do this as quickly and calmly as possible, right? We don't make a move until after the exchange is complete. Then we take him. If there are any problems, we call in the security staff. We don't take any risks. Got it?'

'Got it,' Danny said. 'I'll go page Bryson. Good luck, guys!' He ran ahead.

Just as they were about to come out into the Arrivals area, Maddie faltered.

Alex looked at her. 'Something wrong?'

She stared at him. Her eyes showed her fear. 'What if I mess it up?' she asked hoarsely.

'You'll be fine,' Alex said calmly. 'Just think of it as a performance – like when you used to dance on stage. It's no different. You can do it, Maddie.'

'Aren't you scared?' she asked him.

A wry smile touched his lips. 'Who – me?'

Maddie managed to smile back. 'OK,' she said. 'Just first-night nerves – stage fright, eh?'

Alex nodded.

His steady gaze helped to calm her. And with a long, deep breath, Maddie followed Alex out into the Arrivals area.

Chapter Eight

Maddie swallowed hard as she saw a well-dressed man approach the desk. When he saw Alex and Maddie, he stretched out a hand in greeting. He looked calm and relaxed, as if this was just an ordinary business meeting. Maddie found it hard to believe that he was a close associate of Michael Stone, the man who had destroyed her family.

Alex was quick to take his hand. 'Richard?'

The man nodded. 'Henry. Good to meet you at last.' The hand reached towards Maddie. 'And you must be Grace.'

For an instant, Maddie stared at the hand without moving. Then, with a supreme effort, she shook the man's hand. His grip was warm and firm. A businessman's handshake.

'I was sorry to hear that you were ill,' Richard Bryson said to her. 'Are you feeling better now? Is there anything I can do?'

'I'm much better, thank you,' Maddie said in her American accent. She smiled wanly. 'I'm not a great flyer, Richard. Maybe I should stick to sea crossings from now on.'

Richard laughed. 'Maybe you should.' He glanced at his watch. 'It's been a long day. I'm sure that we all want to get this over with as quickly as possible.' He looked at them. 'Of course you understand I shall need to see the merchandise...'

'Yes, of course,' Maddie said, indicating the handbag.

Richard nodded. 'Excellent.' He ushered them away from the Information Desk.

As they walked with him along the concourse, Danny watched from behind the desk, checking that Bryson had come on his own and ready to call for reinforcements if necessary.

'Where are we going?' Alex asked. Bryson seemed to be heading straight for the exit doors.

'Somewhere a little more private,' Bryson said. 'I'm sure none of us wants to do this in public.'

'Do you have the money?' Maddie asked, looking at Bryson's briefcase.

A flicker of irritation passed over Bryson's suave face. Then he smiled. 'Not on me, Grace,' he said. 'My discussions with Henry, here, made it clear that very large amounts of cash were involved.'

He opened a door and led them out into the floodlit night. Cars and coaches were coming and going. They walked along a sheltered paved area.

'Where's your car?' Alex asked. It seemed obvious now that Bryson was leading them to a vehicle he had waiting.

The smile came again. 'My car?' he said. 'I think I can do better than that, Henry.'

They came to a corner. Bryson stretched out an arm. A few hundred metres away, a helicopter stood on a tarmac pad. 'I don't think there's any fear of us being disturbed while we do business,' he said, then beckoned them on. 'Shall we?'

Alarm bells rang in Alex's head. They had made contingency plans in case things went wrong. Danny had security on standby. There were people at the airport exits, ready to stop any car. But how do you stop a helicopter?

It was obvious that Maddie was thinking along the

same lines. She paused, staring at the sleek, gleaming metallic-blue aircraft. Every light in the airport seemed to be shining in its brightly polished hull, flashing a warning.

'I'm not going up in that,' she said haughtily, thinking fast. 'I've only just recovered from my flight over here in a regular airplane!'

'Don't worry, Grace,' Bryson said. 'No one's going to fly you anywhere. We just sit in there – do our business – and that's it. I fly out – you two go and do whatever else you came here to do. Everyone's happy. OK?'

Maddie looked at the helicopter. They really had no choice. 'OK, I guess so.'

Bryson smiled, then led them across the tarmac.

✪

Danny watched from the corner of the building. The helicopter was as big a shock to him as it had been to Maddie and Alex.

He spoke into his mobile. The frequency was open to allow him to place messages straight into Alex's ear. 'Be careful out there,' he said. 'Don't take any risks. If things get tricky, back off. Cough if you hear me.'

A single, short cough came through his mobile. Alex could hear him. Danny just hoped that Alex would take his advice. It wouldn't be wise to underestimate Richard Bryson.

There was a pilot at the controls of the helicopter. Bryson acknowledged him with a brief wave before opening the wide passenger door. Two pairs of seats faced each other.

'Just put your cases on the floor in here for now,' Bryson said. 'There's plenty of room.' He stepped up into the cabin.

Alex and Maddie glanced at one another. Each knew exactly what the other was thinking. Was this sensible? Was this sane?

Bryson rested his briefcase on his lap. Maddie stepped up and sat in the seat diagonally opposite him. Alex entered last and took the seat next to Bryson.

'There now,' Bryson said calmly. 'Everyone happy?'

Maddie nodded curtly.

'I'll only be happy when this is over with,' Alex said.

'Then I suggest you show me what you've got,' said Bryson.

Maddie opened her handbag and took out the felt pouch. Richard Bryson opened his briefcase. Alex noticed a laptop – some documents – a set of immaculate silver pens – and something wrapped in silky black material.

Bryson slipped a black velvet board out of the lid of the briefcase. He took the pouch from Maddie and carefully spilled the diamonds on to the board.

'So, what have we here?' he said, rolling the diamonds with a single extended finger. 'They're rounds. Judging by the size, between 2.5 and 3.5 carats each.'

He took a small pair of tweezers and an eye-piece from the case. Fitting the eye-piece into the socket of his right eye, he picked up one of the diamonds and held it close to his face.

'D to F grade in colour,' he said. 'Nice. No obvious flaws. The cut quality is very good. Plenty of fire. Nice crown, good pavilion. Good girdle.' He put the diamond down and let the eye-piece fall into his palm. He was smiling. 'Great,' he said. 'I'd price that little fellow at about fifteen thousand pounds. If they're all of a similar quality, I think we can do business.'

He leaned back and rapped his knuckles against the partition that divided the cabin from the cockpit. There was a loud growl that sent a shudder through the helicopter. The pilot had engaged the engine.

'Would someone like to close the door, please?' Bryson said smoothly. 'I wouldn't want anyone falling out.'

'What's going on?' Alex snapped.

'Keep calm, my friend,' Bryson said, still smiling. 'You didn't think I'd risk bringing the money here, did you?' He shrugged. 'And I'm afraid I lied about not taking you anywhere. We're going for a short ride.'

The helicopter shook as the rotors began to whip around above them. The downdraught swirled through the open cabin.

'I really think someone should close that door!' Bryson shouted against the noise. He held out his hands. 'You have to trust me. It's only a fifteen minute trip.'

A voice rang out sharply in Alex's ear. 'Get out of there! It's too dangerous! Get out, now!'

Danny had heard the engine ignite. He was watching the rotors gather speed.

'Forget it!' Alex shouted to Bryson. 'The deal's off!'

He reached towards Maddie, intending to get them both off the helicopter before Bryson could make any moves to try to stop them.

Bryson slid a hand into his briefcase. His face was as calm and impassive as ever. He picked up the bundle of black silk and drew out a gun. He pointed it at Alex.

'Please don't try to get off,' he shouted above the noise of the rotor blades. 'You might get hurt!'

Maddie stared at the gun in horror. Frozen. Terrified. Swamped by memories of that Sunday night one year ago.

Alex was also shocked by the sudden appearance of the weapon.

'Close the door, please, Henry,' Bryson shouted.

Alex leaned out of the cabin. The maelstrom of whirling air tore at his clothes. He reached for the handle and yanked the door shut. The downdraught stopped immediately and the noise was cut by half.

'That's better,' Bryson said calmly. 'There's no need for anyone to lose their cool. Everything's just fine.'

He knocked again on the partition. There was a change in the tone of the engine. The helicopter lurched as it lifted off. Alex saw the tarmac move slowly away as they rose into the night sky.

He looked at Maddie. She was staring at the gun, her eyes wide with fear.

'OK,' Alex said to Bryson. 'You've made your point. Put that thing away.'

Bryson smiled coldly. 'I hope so, Henry. I really hope so. You see, there's been a slight change to the plans since last we discussed them.'

Alex's eyes narrowed. 'Such as what?'

Bryson smiled again. 'Well, the diamonds are a very

pleasant bonus, I'll admit. But what I'm really interested in now,' his eyes flicked towards Maddie, 'is her.'

Maddie let out a gasp.

Alex tensed. Things were getting out of control. They had unwittingly put themselves into real danger with this man. He had to do something – now!

While Bryson's attention was diverted towards Maddie, Alex made his move. He lunged for the gun. But Bryson moved faster. He ducked aside and, with a fierce, deadly look in his eyes, he thrust his arm forwards like a piston. Driven by vicious speed, the gun cracked up against the side of Alex's head.

Pain exploded through Alex's brain. He saw Bryson's expressionless face for a moment, then everything went black.

Chapter Nine

Danny broke his cover as the helicopter lifted itself slowly into the night. He stood on the helipad, staring up helplessly at the underside of the rising craft, his mobile in one clenched fist. 'Alex!' he shouted into it. 'Ale-e-ex!'

The mobile crackled and roared – all Danny could hear through it was the noise of the helicopter's engine. It drowned everything else out.

The shining aircraft turned its nose to the east and began to move rapidly away. Poleaxed by the sudden turn of events, Danny just stood there, staring at the helicopter's shrinking lights until they were just pinpricks in the dark sky.

Then they were gone. Danny let out a low groan. All the enthusiasm and euphoria of the evening drained away from him. Reality came crashing in. Trying to outsmart Richard Bryson, they had fouled up big time.

Danny's mind was blank. He had no idea what to do next. Alex was already way out of range. The Mobile Surveillance Unit was parked nearby, but by the time he got to it, they'd be too far away for the tracers to register.

'Think!' he spat angrily. 'Come on, genius – what are you gonna do now?' His eyes narrowed as his brain got into gear. 'This is a major airport. Planes are coming and going all the time.' He was muttering to himself. Thinking aloud. 'You can't just fly a helicopter out without checking that you're not going to crash into stuff in mid-air.' His eyes gleamed. 'They must have left a flight plan with Air Traffic Control. That's it!'

He ran towards the building.

It took Danny four frantic minutes and several flashes of his PIC identity card before he found himself in the Duty Manager's office.

The Duty Manager nodded as Danny explained what he needed, and tapped the details into his computer. Seconds later, the information scrolled up on the screen.

'They've been logging provisional flight-plans for the past two hours,' he began. 'Waiting for incoming VIPs, apparently. They're scheduled to make a stop-off in West London – W14 – that's probably Holland Park – and then continue into Essex. A place in Loughton. Near Epping Forest. Both stops are in the grounds of private houses. That's the best I can do.'

'Thanks.' Danny clapped a grateful hand down on the man's shoulder. 'West London. W14. Got it!'

And he raced off for the MSU. He had the lead he needed. Now he had a chance to find Alex and Maddie before really bad things started to happen.

❌

Frozen in shock, Maddie stared at Richard Bryson's gun. His eyes were cold and calm.

'You're not going to do anything silly, are you, Grace?' he asked.

She shook her head. She looked at Alex. He was slumped sideways in his seat, unconscious. There was a raw, red welt at his temple where the gun had struck.

'You shouldn't have done that,' she said. 'You didn't need to hit him that hard.' Terrified as she was, a small clear part of her brain told her to maintain her American accent. Things would only get worse if Richard Bryson discovered who they really were.

'He'll be fine,' Bryson said. 'Strange, Henry didn't strike me as a stupid man. But that was a stupid thing to do.' He frowned. 'I don't like using force on people, Grace, but we're not playing games here.'

Maddie stared into the unreadable face of her captor. 'What do you want with us?' she asked.

Bryson held up the gun. 'Can I put this away now?' he said. 'Am I going to be safe with you?'

She nodded.

The gun went back into its black silk wrap, and Bryson placed it carefully in his briefcase. Maddie didn't fail to notice that it was still within easy reach.

Bryson leaned back and crossed his legs. He looked at her with the lightless, predatory eyes of a shark. 'I'm going to talk to you as one intelligent person to another, Grace,' he said. 'It'll save time. Now, I'm going to start by assuming you know how your father earns most of his money.'

Maddie nodded, but she wondered how much Grace really did know about the criminal side of Patrick O'Connor's empire.

Bryson's manicured fingers touched his chest. 'I work for people in the same line of business. My boss and your father have been negotiating a big deal now for well over a year.' He frowned. 'The talks have been stalled for months. It's a complete stalemate. A real problem. Now, you probably won't know about this, but we're experiencing a bit of trouble over here. My boss was – uh, inconvenienced, shall we say – by an unfortunate event last summer. He had to go away for a while, if you understand what I mean. Ever since then, his son has been running the business. He's also taken over the negotiations with your father.' He looked at her. 'Are you following me so far, Grace?'

'Yes,' Maddie said. 'I don't care about it. I just want you to let us out of here.'

'All in good time,' Bryson said, lifting his hand. He leaned forward and his fingertips touched Maddie's arm. 'I'm going to be absolutely frank with you, Grace, and I hope you won't take offence. The thing is, I'm sick and tired of the stalling. Your father seems to think that because the boss is away, he can rip us off. I think it's about time something was done to break the stalemate – purely in order to get the talks back on track, you understand. And that's where you come in.' He patted Maddie's hand and then leaned back again.

'I look at it like this,' he said. 'Your father is going to be a lot more co-operative when he finds out that you're our house-guest. We're not going to issue any threats – of course not – we're businessmen, Grace, not thugs. We'll just make it clear to your father that if he wants to see you again soon, it would be a good idea for him to start taking us a bit more seriously.'

Maddie's mind was whirling. At least now she had some idea of what was happening. Henry Dean had approached Bryson to fence the diamonds for him. Bryson had agreed, but at some point he'd come up with this double-cross: to kidnap Grace and use her as a bargaining tool to squeeze concessions out of Patrick O'Connor.

But he had made a fatal mistake. Richard Bryson didn't actually have Patrick O'Connor's daughter – he had Maddie Cooper and Alex Cox.

A low moan from Alex broke into Maddie's thoughts.

Bryson reached across and lifted one of Alex's eyelids with his thumb. 'He'll be out for a while yet,' he said. 'It's not good for you – being hit around the head. He'll have one heck of a headache when he wakes up.'

Maddie's face twisted into anger and distaste.

Bryson looked at her. 'You don't approve of what I did,' he observed. 'But let's not be hypocritical, here, Grace,' he continued. 'Your father's hands aren't exactly clean, are they now? You can't pretend you don't know how heavily he has leant on people to make some of his deals.'

Bryson delicately picked out one of the diamonds and held it to his eye. 'I think I can see blood on these bright little sparklers, too, Grace. Or would you rather not think about that? A bit too close to home, maybe, hmm?' Carefully, slowly, one by one, he placed the diamonds back in their felt pouch.

Maddie stared out of the window. Trying to get her thoughts in line. The lights of the city were moving slowly beneath them. They were being taken somewhere not far from the airport. A fifteen minute journey, Bryson had said. Somewhere in West London, then.

There was nothing she could do while they were in the air. She wasn't strong enough to overpower her kidnapper, even if she dared to launch an attack on him. Besides, there was still the gun.

No. She had to sit tight and wait for them to land. Until then, she had to play along – to keep up the charade of being Grace O'Connor. To hope that her disguise didn't slip. Once they were on the ground, there would be a much better chance to get out of this nightmare.

But what might happen if Bryson learned that he had Jack Cooper's daughter in his clutches, Maddie didn't want to consider.

As she looked anxiously at Alex – hoping desperately

that he would be all right – a bleak, ironic thought flitted through her head. *We should have quit work early! If we'd just gone to the gym, none of this would have happened.*

She had got herself and Alex into this desperate situation, and now all she could do was sit helplessly as they flew further and further from Danny, and any chance of rescue.

Chapter Ten

The MSU sped eastwards along the M4. The motorway led from the airport right into the heart of London. The traffic was a continuous stream. At least it was moving, but not quickly enough for Danny.

'Come on! Come on!' he muttered at every touch on the brake. 'Don't you people have anywhere you need to be?' He bounced his fist off the wheel. 'Jeez – it'd be quicker to get out and walk. Move it, guys!'

The back of the MSU was crammed with cutting-edge surveillance equipment, most of which was not yet in the public domain. Danny had been like a kid in a candy store installing it all and checking that it worked correctly. There were even a few devices he'd dreamed up himself. There was just one problem. The MSU had been designed to be operated by two people: one driving, the other working the equipment.

Danny was on his own. This had all started off as a routine immigration exercise for him. No one had expected things to escalate like this. Danny couldn't drive and make the trace on Maddie and Alex at the same time. He drove, or he tracked them. One or the other. And right now, his priority was to get the van into West London and hope that he could pick them up on the stop-off in W14. If Maddie and Alex were still on board when the helicopter took off for Essex, then they were in big trouble.

Danny's mobile was lying beside him on the passenger seat, but the noise of the helicopter engine was drowning everything else out. So far, he'd avoided calling for help. He still clung to a shred of hope that everything would work out OK. If only he could get to Holland Park in time.

He resisted the urge to lean on the horn.

'Chill out, Danny,' he muttered to himself. 'Everything's gonna work out fine. The guy is just taking them someplace to do the swap. He'd have been crazy to take the money to Heathrow.' He nodded, convincing himself. 'The chopper will touch down and the guys will get off. They'll do the business, and Alex and Maddie will arrest Bryson. End of story. And if there's any trouble, I'll be right there to back 'em up.'

Danny hoped it wouldn't come to that. He wasn't a hard man like Alex. Physical stuff wasn't his speciality. He always left the self-defence classes bruised and aching.

'Not that there's gonna be any trouble,' Danny said to himself. 'Everything's gonna be real cool.' Ahead of him he saw the Hogarth roundabout. Things would slow down even more now. But once he got past the Hammersmith flyover, it shouldn't take him more than fifteen minutes to hit Holland Park.

He didn't want to think about how far a helicopter could have flown in that time.

❌

Maddie stared out of the helicopter's window as night-lit London rolled beneath them. She could see the motorway, a broad, dark strip filled with thousands of moving lights. She hoped Danny's van was down there somewhere.

She glanced at Richard Bryson. The briefcase was resting upright on the floor beside him; the gun still within easy reach. Not that he needed it. Maddie felt sick. Richard Bryson, I am arresting you for possession of stolen diamonds... That was some joke!

They had hoped to pick Bryson off as easy as swatting a fly. Maddie had never imagined that things could have gone so badly wrong. All she could do now was to play along and hope the pair of them came out of this in one piece.

Poor Alex. He was still out of it, his body slumped against the side of the cabin, his head lolling to the sway of the helicopter.

A dark expanse opened up beneath them. Maddie didn't know it, but they were flying over Gunnersbury Park. They had come into the western outskirts of London. They were getting close to their destination.

'Where are you taking us?' Maddie asked, unable to bear Bryson's silence any longer. She didn't expect him to answer, but if she could only get him talking, maybe he'd accidentally let something slip that she could use.

Bryson looked up at her. 'A little place we own,' he said. A faint smile lifted his lip. 'Don't worry. You'll be quite comfortable there.'

'Will Eddie Stone be there?' she asked.

Richard Bryson looked at her for a while without speaking. 'Does your father discuss his business with you?' he asked.

Maddie was puzzled by the question. 'No.'

Bryson's eyebrows raised. 'So, how do you know about Eddie Stone?' he asked.

'You must have mentioned his name,' Maddie said. Cold sweat ran down her spine. Her stomach knotted. In trying to out-think Richard Bryson, she realised that she may have put herself in a trap.

Bryson shook his head. 'No,' he said, 'I never mentioned his name.'

'Then it must have been Henry,' Maddie said. 'Henry must have said something about him.' She masked her fear with fake anger. 'How the heck should I know where I heard the guy's name? Who cares, anyway?'

Bryson looked thoughtfully at Alex. 'Your boyfriend has a big mouth,' he said slowly. 'It could land him in trouble.'

'Oh, right!' said Maddie. 'Like, we're not in trouble now!' She tried another tack. 'Listen, Richard, can't we come to some kind of arrangement here?'

Bryson gazed impassively at her. 'Go on,' he said.

'If you let Henry and I go, you can keep the diamonds,' she said. Maddie was trying to get them free, but in the back of her mind she remembered Danny slipping that tracer into the felt pouch. The diamonds could still be used to nail Bryson.

'And?' Bryson said.

She glared at him. 'And what?' she said. 'And Henry and I walk away, and you get to keep several hundred thousand dollars' worth of diamonds.' She allowed a slyness to creep into her voice. 'And your boss need never know what happened. You won't even have to share the profits.'

Bryson smiled. 'Forget it, Grace,' he said. 'You've got nothing to negotiate with. For a start, I already have the diamonds. And as for the rest of your plan, the thing is that I want Eddie to know about this. That's the whole point.'

Maddie frowned. Eddie Stone was Michael Stone's eldest son. He had stepped in as acting CEO of Stonecor when his father had been put out of circulation. Maddie didn't know much about him, except that he was in his mid-twenties, and as squeaky-clean as his father had been right up until Jack Cooper had arrested him in the Diamond Depository. Meaning that Eddie Stone was probably as big a crook as his father, except that, as yet, there was nothing to prove it.

Maddie had seen the files on Stonecor. They owned a string of houses, offices and warehouses all over London. Every known property had been thoroughly searched at the time of Michael Stone's arrest. The police had drawn a blank. There had not been one shred of evidence linking Stonecor to Stone's criminal activities. Not one box of stolen goods. Not one computer file. Not one piece of paper.

'So, you're just going to hand us and the diamonds over to Eddie Stone,' Maddie said. 'Way to lose a small fortune, Richard.'

Bryson laughed softly. 'Don't worry about it, Grace. I'll be gaining more than I lose.' He glanced out of the window. 'Ah!' he said. 'We're almost there.' He looked at Alex. 'Your boyfriend missed the whole ride,' he said. 'Pity. Things are so much easier when people co-operate.'

'And when they don't, you resort to violence,' Maddie said, looking meaningfully at Alex.

'Violence?' Bryson said. 'That wasn't violence. That was just a gentle tap on the head. He'll soon get over it.' His eyes went dead as he looked at her. 'When I'm forced to use violence, Grace, people don't recover so quickly.' His voice was completely emotionless. 'Sometimes,' he said, 'people don't recover at all.'

Chapter Eleven

In the wealthy West London area of Holland Park, a smartly dressed woman stood beside the open French windows of a large, detached house. It occupied a corner plot, plaster-clad and painted white, one of a whole row of huge Victorian buildings owned by millionaires and embassies. Its east-facing grounds were enclosed by a high white wall. Tall trees pointed towards the night sky. A stone patio led down to a smooth, flat lawn.

The woman was speaking into a mobile and watching the sky. 'Yes,' she said, 'everything's ready, Mr Bryson. Everything has been dealt with. I spoke to Mr Stone half an hour ago. He's hoping to get here sometime tomorrow morning.' There was a pause. 'Excuse me,' she said. 'Could you repeat that?' Her face didn't alter as she listened to Richard Bryson's voice.

'Yes,' she said. 'Yes, I understand. I'll organise it.'

She cut the line. She walked into the house. Henry Dean was apparently unconscious. She needed to find someone to fetch him out of the helicopter. These were not unusual circumstances for the woman. She'd known worse in the five years she'd worked for Stonecor. Much worse.

○

Maddie watched the rooftops rising to meet them. She couldn't believe that they would be able to land safely here. There wouldn't be enough room.

Richard Bryson pocketed his mobile and sat back.

Tall treetops thrashed about as the helicopter came down in the garden of a huge white house. Long chimney stacks rose from the roof. Abstractedly, Maddie counted the chimneypots of one stack. Seventeen.

The house was three storeys high. Square and solid. Ornamental brickwork cornices ran around the building at the intersection of each floor, making the house look like an iced layer-cake. It dominated the intersection of two roads. At the back, security lights shone bright pools down on a stone patio. Trees rimmed a lawn. Maddie felt slightly dizzy as she looked down.

The engine noise changed as the pilot brought the helicopter down towards the lawn. Its steel runners hit the ground with a thump.

'There,' Bryson said. 'All over.' He frowned in a semblance of concern. 'You didn't feel air-sick, did you?'

Maddie shook her head.

'Excellent,' Bryson said. He smiled. 'Now, would you open the door for me? It'll save me climbing all over poor old Henry, here.'

Maddie pushed at the lever and the door opened. Something pulled it out of her hand. A rush of air and bits of grass and leaves filled the cabin, along with the redoubled roar of the spinning rotors. A woman was crouched in the doorway. She beckoned to Maddie.

Maddie climbed down. A tall, heavily built man was waiting there.

He pulled Alex effortlessly out of the helicopter, dragging him along the lawn until they were away from the swirl of the rotors. Then he hoisted Alex on to his shoulder and marched off with him towards the house.

Richard Bryson handed Grace and Henry's cases to

the woman who was standing beside Maddie. He stepped out on to the lawn, bending low to avoid the scything rotors. He slammed the door. The helicopter pilot made a thumbs-up gesture and the machine roared back up into the sky.

The grass swirled like green water. The trees quivered as the helicopter lifted above the rooftops.

As the noise began to diminish, the woman turned to Maddie. 'Miss O'Connor, how are you feeling?' she asked. 'Mr Bryson told me you were taken ill on the plane. Are you feeling better now?' Maddie looked at her. She had all the appearance and manner of a personal assistant.

'My friend needs to see a doctor,' Maddie said frostily. 'He's been hurt.'

'We'll do everything we can to make him comfortable,' said the woman. 'Please? Would you come into the house?' She smiled. 'I'm Celia – Celia Thomson, Mr Stone's PA. If there's anything you want – anything at all – you just have to ask. We want to make your stay here as pleasant as possible. Think of yourself as our guest.'

'Quit the friendly act,' Maddie snapped, in an attempt to behave as she thought Grace would, but also out of her own anger and fear. 'I'm not a guest here!' She glared at Richard Bryson. 'I'm a prisoner!'

Bryson smiled. 'Make it easy on yourself, Grace,' he said. 'Don't fight us. It's really not worth it.' He turned and walked towards the house, leaving the two suitcases standing in the grass.

Maddie stared after him. 'You're going to regret this!' she hissed between her teeth.

Celia Thomson lifted the two suitcases and followed Bryson. She looked around at Maddie. 'We really will do everything we can to make you comfortable, Miss O'Connor,' she said. 'Please, come in. It's getting cold.' An eyebrow rose. 'You're hardly dressed for a chilly London night, are you?'

Maddie hesitated. Between the trees, she could see sections of a high white wall. It ran right around the garden. There was a narrow alley up the side of the building, but the wall lights showed a barred door at the far end.

She thought it unlikely that she would be able to get through that door, or to scale that garden wall. Besides, she couldn't leave Alex the way he was.

Bryson had gone in through the French windows. Celia Thomson was standing in the doorway, silhouetted against the light. Looking back at Maddie. Waiting.

Maddie took her time. She smoothed her dress

down, carefully checking that the tracer tape was still there under the hem. Then she walked slowly towards the house.

The room was starkly modern: cream walls, bleached, bare floorboards, partially covered with intricately woven rugs; furniture all pale wood, glass and leather.

'Welcome,' Celia said, smiling.

Maddie gave her a withering look. 'None of this impresses me, you know,' she said softly. 'Behind all this upmarket style, you're just a bunch of thugs, if you want my opinion.'

Celia's smile didn't waver. 'I'm so glad you feel able to speak your mind like that,' she said. 'I know this can't be easy for you. I sympathise, I really do. We're all finding this situation difficult. But we just have to try to make the best of it. Can I show you to your room?'

Maddie shook her head. 'I want to know how Henry is,' she said, standing stubbornly in the middle of the floor. 'If he's badly hurt, my father will see that you pay for it. I can promise you that.'

'Yes, of course,' Celia said. 'We should see how he's getting on.' She put down the cases and moved to the French windows. 'Let's shut the night out, shall we?' She closed the doors and turned a key. 'I know it's spring, but there can still be quite a bite to the air once it gets dark. What kind of weather were you having in Boston, Miss O'Connor?'

Maddie didn't reply.

There was a security box behind the white curtain. Celia tapped out a series of numbers. 'There,' she said. 'All secure.' She smiled around at Maddie. 'You can't be too careful. Burglaries have gone up seventeen per cent this year. Isn't that terrible? People aren't safe in their own homes any more. And we have some quite valuable equipment here.' She closed the curtains. 'Now then,' she said. 'Why don't you make yourself at home, while I go and find out how your friend is doing?'

Maddie found herself alone in the room. Her head was whirling. She felt like she'd fallen into some unpredictable, twisted world where anything could happen.

Maddie understood that she had to tread very carefully among these people. This house was a snake pit, and one wrong move could prove disastrous. Above all, she had to keep up the pretence of being Grace O'Connor. So long as they believed that she was Patrick O'Connor's daughter, they would be unlikely to harm her – she was too valuable to them.

But that meant Alex had to keep his act up, too. He had to be with-it enough to maintain his role as Henry Dean when he regained consciousness, or the whole thing would come crashing down around their ears.

Maddie's main fear was that a groggy Alex, waking up with a throbbing head – disorientated – woozy from the blow Bryson had inflicted upon him – might speak in an English accent which would ruin everything.

What would Richard Bryson do if he discovered that his 'guests' were with the police? He might even decide that the safest course would be to get rid of them both. Permanently.

Maddie felt dizzy with fear. *Danny! You've got to find us,* she thought, *and get us out of here.*

The door opened. Celia leaned into the room.

'Good news, Miss O'Connor,' she said. 'Mr Dean is waking up. It looks like he's going to be just fine.' She smiled. 'Mr Bryson is with him now. Your friend was trying to say something a few moments ago but I'm afraid he's still feeling a little groggy.'

'I guess you'd feel groggy if you'd been hit with a gun,' Maddie snapped. 'I want to see him. Now!'

'Well, of course you do,' said Celia. 'You must be terribly worried about him. Let me take you to him.'

Maddie followed Celia out into a broad white

hallway. A flight of pale marble stairs swept upwards in a long, gentle curve. The woman's heels clicked sharply on the stone as she ascended.

As they reached the top, Celia looked around. 'Once you've assured yourself that Mr Dean is doing fine, there'll just be time for you to freshen up before supper. I hope you like Italian food,' she said, the smile appearing yet again.

Maddie was beginning to loathe that smile.

They began to ascend a second flight of stairs. Bryson appeared suddenly at the top. He stood there, his arms folded, staring down at Maddie as she climbed.

'Your friend is awake,' he said, his eyes dark and hard. A cruel smile touched his lips. 'He's just said something very interesting.' He gestured towards a half-open door along the hallway. 'Maybe you'd like to come and hear it for yourself. It puts a whole new light on the situation we have here.'

Chapter Twelve

The MSU was parked halfway up Blythe Road, off the Hammersmith Road by Olympia. Danny was crouched in the back among all the electronic gear. The scanner screen was in operation. It glowed green. A faint beep sounded every few seconds. Picking up nothing.

Danny was staring intently at a street map. W14 covered about a square kilometre of tangled streets. It wouldn't have been an impossibly huge area for Danny to check; not if he had plenty of time, and a driver to cruise the van through the streets while he tinkered away in the back.

But he didn't have time. And there was no one else

to help him. He was working alone and against the clock. His greatest fear was that in his desperate urgency to find Alex and Maddie, he might miss something. More haste, less speed. He had to keep cool. He had to keep focused. He had to find them quickly.

In an open field, the equipment he had in the van could pick the tracer up at 200 metres. But in winding London streets, where all the houses had some kind of electrical appliances, and most had high-frequency electronic security systems, picking the weak tracer signal out of all that background interference was going to be a long and frustrating business.

Danny ran his finger along the muddle of streets on the map. Why couldn't London be more like Chicago? Straight lines. Square blocks. This place was just one big mess.

The only large open area on the map was the green rectangle of Holland Park. Any halfway decent pilot could bring the chopper down there. But air traffic control had said the chopper was due to stop off on private property. As far as Danny knew, Holland Park wasn't privately owned. So the chopper had to come down somewhere else. OK. Options. Right in the middle of Kensington High Street? No way. Not even the Brits were crazy enough to try that. On a rooftop pad, maybe? Say, the Kensington Roof Gardens? Unlikely. In the grounds of some big house? Almost definitely.

But where? Danny needed to make a choice – and fast. Holland Road ran down the centre of the area – there was one mess of streets to the west, and another bunch to the east.

Which was it to be? East or west?

'Well, smart boy, you're on the west right now,' he murmured to himself. 'I guess you might as well stay here.' He took a red pen and mapped out a route that would take in every street. Now that he was moving through relatively quiet side streets, he'd be able to hear the steady, monotonous beep of the scanner from the driver's seat. The moment that note changed, he'd have them.

Danny clambered over the back of the driver's seat and prepared himself for a long haul. If Maddie and Alex were in the area, he was going to find them, even if it took him till daybreak.

He talked to himself to keep his spirits up. Underneath, he was seriously concerned for Alex and Maddie's safety. A man like Richard Bryson might pretend to be nothing more than a regular businessman, but if the guys made one wrong move, things could turn ugly very quickly. Danny just hoped that they had the sense to stay in character.

Richard Bryson would not be happy if he found out he'd brought a couple of wannabe undercover cops home with him.

❌

Maddie was led into a bedroom. It was furnished in the same, minimal style as the room downstairs. Alex was sitting up on a large double bed. His face looked grey against the white cover – except for the dark red weal left by the impact of the gun on the side of his face.

Alex glowered at Maddie. The cold anger in his eyes shocked her for a moment.

'Get her out of here,' Alex said. 'I told you – I don't want to see her.' He was still using the American accent. Maddie quickly realised that Alex was play-acting. He must have a plan.

'I think you should see her, Henry,' Bryson said. 'I think Grace deserves to hear what you just told me.'

Alex looked at her. He had obviously been studying Richard Bryson, because his eyes were as cold and dead as Bryson's as he looked at her. 'The way I see it, Grace,' he drawled, his voice flat and emotionless, 'it's you these people want – not me. Well, baby, as far as

I'm concerned, they can have you – just so long as they let me out of here.'

Maddie understood immediately that she had to react convincingly to this. The real Grace would be hurt and horrified by her boyfriend's brutal betrayal.

'You rat!' she hissed, eyes blazing. 'How could you?' She made a move towards the bed.

Bryson's arm flicked out and his left hand closed lightly around her wrist. 'Calm down, Grace. Let's not get hysterical.'

She glared at him. 'Hysterical?' she cried. She looked at Alex. 'I trusted you! I thought you cared about me!'

'I cared about the diamonds,' Alex said coldly. 'You were just an easy way for me to get to them.' He shrugged. 'The game's over, Gracie. I'm out of here.' He climbed off the bed. Slightly unsteady on his feet. Still giddy. Head throbbing. Determined to play his part convincingly enough to be set free. He could do a lot more for Maddie once he was out of that house, more than he could ever do from within.

Richard Bryson reached his hand out to Alex. 'No hard feelings, I hope,' he said.

'None at all,' Alex replied, shaking the offered hand. 'I'm just glad we've come to an amicable arrangement.' He looked at Maddie. 'Bye, Grace. I'll see you around, maybe.'

'Not if I see you first!' Maddie spat. It was going to work! Alex was going to be set free. Everything would be all right.

Alex walked towards the door.

'Shall I have Celia call you a taxi?' Bryson asked.

'No. I'll be fine. Thanks.'

'What are your plans, Henry?' Bryson asked.

Alex turned in the doorway. He had to play it cool. 'I have a plane ticket to Switzerland,' he said. 'I guess I'll go use it.'

'A moment, please,' Bryson said.

Alex looked at him.

Bryson shook his head. 'Sorry, Henry. I can't let you go. It was a nice try, but I'm not buying it.'

Alex stared at him. 'What are you talking about, Richard? I thought we had a deal, here. You keep the girl – I keep my mouth shut.'

'And you walk away from this whole thing without a penny?' Bryson said, smiling, shaking his head. 'I'm sorry, Henry. It won't wash. If you were really as cold-blooded as you'd like me to believe, you'd have wanted your share of the diamonds. You've risked everything to get this far – you wouldn't walk away from a quarter of a million without a word.'

'You think I'm lying?' Alex said.

'Of course you're lying, Henry,' Bryson replied. 'You're not going to run out on Grace. You care too much about her. You're not a fool, Henry. You knew the deal was going bad from the moment we got into the helicopter. You could have got clear on your own while the door was still open – but you wanted to take Grace with you.' He spread his hands. 'Now, tell me, Henry, is that the act of a man who doesn't give a damn about his girl? Of course it isn't. And what are you going to do if I let you out of here? You're going to do everything you can to get Grace out, too.' Bryson's voice lowered to a dangerous growl. 'You might even decide to go to the police, Henry. You might even do something as foolish as that.' He shook his head. 'I can't allow it, Henry. I'm sorry. You're staying put.'

Alex hesitated for a moment, as if he didn't know what to do. But when he did move, he moved with lightning speed and ferocity. Bracing himself in the doorway, he lashed out at Bryson with a waist-high martial arts kick.

Bryson was taken completely by surprise. Alex's practised blow struck him in the side, doubling him up and sending him crashing to the carpet. Celia Thomson let out a yell.

A moment later, a huge shape blocked the doorway at Alex's back. It was the thug who had carried Alex from the helicopter. His massive fist came down like a hammer. Alex crumpled to his knees. Great, meaty hands bore down on his shoulders, a knee thumped into the small of his back, pinning him to the floor.

It was all over almost before Maddie had the time to react.

Richard Bryson staggered to his feet, his clothes dishevelled, his face thunderous with anger and pain. He clutched his side. His eyes were venomous.

'Thank you... Jack...' he gasped. 'I think Mr Dean... needs to be taught... a lesson in manners.' He gestured towards the bed. 'Soften him up. I'll be back to deal with him later.'

Maddie watched in horror as the big thug hauled Alex to his feet and threw him across the room.

'Don't hurt him!' she cried. 'Please. Don't hurt him!'

Richard Bryson's veneer of courtesy had been ripped away by Alex's attack. He grasped Maddie by the neck and pushed her out into the hallway. As the door slammed on Alex, she heard the sound of a fist being driven home. There was a single stifled groan.

Alex was paying dearly for his attempt to escape.

Chapter Thirteen

Maddie sat at the immense dining-room table. Her only companion was Celia Thomson. The woman was eating with the precision of a bird. Pecking at her food.

Maddie hadn't eaten a bite. She was sick with worry about Alex. She hadn't seen him for over an hour now – not since Richard Bryson had thrown her out of that upstairs bedroom. She had spent most of that time alone in the sitting room. Locked in. Fearing the worst. Then Celia had come to fetch her for the meal.

'Aren't you hungry, Miss O'Connor?' Celia asked, looking up at Maddie.

Maddie ignored her question. 'Where's Henry?' she asked.

'He'll be eating in his room, I'm afraid,' Celia replied. 'Mr Bryson thinks it's safer that way. He's concerned that Mr Dean might... well – you know.' She nodded and gave Maddie a faint smile. 'It's better to be on the safe side, don't you think? Mr Dean could get badly hurt if he isn't more careful.'

Maddie stared at her. 'What is it with you?' she said. 'Are you stupid or insane or what?' Celia gave her a surprised look. 'You act like – like this is all OK. Like this is all perfectly normal.' Her voice rose. 'I'm being held prisoner here. My friend has been beaten up. And you act like this is all just everyday stuff. Are you out of your mind?'

Celia looked at her. 'It's good that you're able to express your anger so forcefully,' she said with infuriating calmness. 'I expect I'd be upset, too, if I was in your position. But this is all just business, Miss O'Connor. You have to understand that. None of it is personal. If Mr Dean had behaved himself, no one would have laid a finger on him. But he has to learn that he mustn't cause trouble.' She fished thoughtfully through her food with a slender silver fork. 'What we do is no different from what people do in business all over the world. Our way is just a little more... direct, that's all.' She waved a hand. 'Oh, I suppose we cut corners, sometimes,' she said. 'And we have a more straightforward way of dealing with problems than you might find in other places – but the basic principal is the same. Our job is to keep ahead of the competition, and to make a profit. It's as simple as that.'

The quiet, reasonable way in which Celia spoke, made her words all the more chilling to Maddie. If she really believed all that, then she was as bad as Richard Bryson. Worse, maybe.

'Is Henry OK?' Maddie asked in a subdued voice.

'He's fine,' Celia said. 'He seems a tough young man. He'll have a few bruises, but nothing that won't mend in a few days.' She smiled. 'And who knows, if our negotiations with your father work out the way we all hope they will, the two of you might be out of here in a couple of days. I hear you're running away together. That is just so romantic. I'd love to hear all about it.'

Maddie stared at her in disbelief. 'Do you really think I'm going to sit here making polite conversation with you,' she said, 'when I'm sure that if I made trouble, you'd give me the same treatment as your boss gave Henry?'

'Not at all,' Celia said. 'I wouldn't know how to hit you, even if I wanted to.' She smiled. 'Eat your food, Miss O'Connor. You don't want to make yourself ill.'

She was right. Maddie realised that she had to eat. She needed to keep her strength up and her wits about her. That was her only chance of coming out of this ordeal in one piece.

Her stomach churned as she put food in her mouth. She chewed slowly. She had no appetite. She forced the food down in grim silence.

'Good,' Celia said, nodding approvingly at Maddie's empty plate. 'Well done.' She sipped from her wineglass. 'Now then, how would you like to spend the rest of the evening? We could maybe watch a movie. We have quite a large selection of DVDs. What kind of movies do you like?'

Maddie looked icily at her. 'Do you have any gangster movies?' she said. 'I'd really like to watch a good, old-fashioned one where all the villains wind up in prison at the end.'

Celia gave her a pained look. 'Ouch!' she said. 'But it's good to see that you're getting your sense of humour back, Miss O'Connor.'

Maddie shrugged. 'It's easy when you're dealing with such nice people.' Her eyes were cold. 'So, are we going to sit up chatting all night?' she asked tartly.

Celia patted her mouth with a linen napkin. 'Of course, you must be tired,' she said. 'This must have been a very trying day for you. I'll show you to your room.' The smile returned. 'A good night's sleep will make all the difference. You'll see.'

She led Maddie up to the second floor. Maddie paused, staring at the door of the room where Alex was being held.

'Now come along, Miss O'Connor,' Celia said. 'Let's not bother Mr Dean.' She opened a door, two along from Alex's room.

The room was decorated with the same minimalism as the rest of the house. Grace O'Connor's suitcase lay on the bed.

Celia opened an inner door to show Maddie the *en suite* bathroom, then pointed to a shelf unit. 'Books and magazines, if you want to read – and a TV if you can't sleep. There's a bell push by the bed. Just press it if you need anything.'

Maddie looked at the window. 'A rope ladder would be useful,' she said.

Celia laughed politely, then moved towards the door. 'We're looking after your mobile, by the way, in case you wonder where it's gone.'

Celia turned one last time in the doorway. 'Goodnight, Miss O'Connor. Sleep well.'

Maddie fixed her with a piercing look. 'When my father finds out about this,' she said with slow precision, 'you will all regret this. Just remember I told you so.'

'Thank you. I'll bear that in mind,' Celia replied. Then she closed the door.

Maddie heard the click of a key in the lock. Her defiant look faded at the sound. At the moment she had made it, the threat had sounded very real to her. Certainly, when Jack Cooper found out what had happened to his daughter, he'd rip London's underworld wide open to find her.

When he found out. But when would that be?

Jack Cooper was at the Economic Summit, and the only person in the world who had any idea of what had happened was Danny. And what chance did he have of finding them? A tracer that had a range of 200 metres in a city thirteen miles across. No chance. No chance at all...

Maddie slumped on to the bed, her face in her hands. All her bravado was gone. She collapsed on to the cool white sheets, her head cradled in her arms.

She had never felt so utterly exhausted and alone.

✪

Danny looked at his watch. It was past midnight. He knuckled his eyes. He wasn't tired – the adrenaline flowing through his body kept him wide awake – but his senses were becoming blurred from the constant strain.

The painstaking quartering of the block of streets to the west of Holland Road had revealed nothing. Now the MSU was parked in Somerset Square, and Danny was taking a few moments out to mark up the map for a whole new search. There were fewer streets to the east of Holland Road. The houses were bigger. The roads were full of Porsches, Maseratis and four-wheel drives. The whole area oozed wealth and privilege.

The scanner beeped.

Danny looked at the device. The unchanging noise was beginning to tell on his nerves. He frowned, stabbing a finger towards the monitor.

'Now, listen here,' he growled. 'I didn't spend three days putting you together for you just to sit there going beep, right? Now, what I want from you in the next few minutes are a lot of bip-bip-bip noises.' He glared at the green screen. 'Get the picture? Good! Then let's go.'

He manoeuvred the van out into the road. The

tree-lined streets were quiet and still. Every now and then a single car would come purring past with a brief flash of headlights. Apart from that, Danny felt creepily alone – as though all the world was asleep except for him.

He strained to hear the dull beep of the scanner over the noise of the van's motor.

'Wish I'd brought a flask of coffee,' he muttered to himself. 'I could use some caffeine right now.' He steered the van around a corner. Across the street, the sign read Addison Road. He turned right and cruised slowly along the dark road.

About two-thirds of the way along the road something strange happened in the back of the van. The sound of the scanner was suddenly drowned out by a wall of white noise. Danny frowned. Puzzled. He carried on driving. The loud hissing continued for about five seconds, and then faded.

Beep. Beep. Beep.

He had heard similar noises on and off all night. It was interference from security systems, breaking into the frequency he was using and scrambling the signal. But he hadn't come across a white noise that powerful before. Somewhere along that road was a house with one mother of a security field around it. Not just a regular anti-burglar system: this was something much bigger.

Danny drove along to a side road. He turned the van and headed back the way he had come. He crawled along at 10 mph. Listening out for the noise.

He passed another side street. There was a big white house on the corner.

The hissing came back even stronger. As Danny passed the side of the white house, it rose to a crescendo.

Danny searched for somewhere to park. He was in luck. There was a single space on the far side of the road. He slid into it and cut the motor.

He crawled into the back of the van. He adjusted several faders and touch-sensitive pads. The white noise faded a little.

He frowned, crouching intently over the electronic devices, concentrating hard, trying to filter out the unwanted interference.

A hidden sound emerged.

Bip-bip-bip-bip-bip.

Danny's eyes widened. A grin spread across his face.

'At last!' he whispered, hardly daring to believe what he was hearing from the scanner. 'Danny, you boy-genius, you've only gone and found them!'

His head fell forwards and he began to laugh in exhausted relief.

It was 12:28 Now all he had to do was get them out...

Chapter Fourteen

Maddie restlessly prowled her room like a caged tiger. End to end. Door to window. She should have been tired. She should have been dead on her feet. But something kept pumping energy into her limbs. Fear. And anger. Desperation. Concern about Alex. All those things. Her mind was churning.

She walked to the tall, sash window and drew the curtains open. She looked down into the dark well of the garden. Shards of the white wall gleamed between the trees. She opened the window as quietly as she could and leaned out. The air was chilly. The grey stones of the patio lay ten metres beneath her. Far too long a jump. She didn't dare. She'd break bones. Or worse.

A cornice ran along the wall about a metre beneath her window. It was no more than ten centimetres wide.

Maddie looked to the side. There were two more tall windows in that section of wall. One window per room. That meant the second window belonged to the room where Alex was being kept.

Towering above all other thoughts in Maddie's mind was the desire to make contact with Alex. Even if only to let him know she was all right. To reassure him that everything would turn out fine.

Danny will be here any time now – don't worry.

Except that she didn't really believe that. She believed that they were on their own.

Maddie turned and walked to the door. She stared at the handle. She had heard Celia turn the key. She knew she was locked in. She gripped the handle and twisted it. The door stayed put.

A burst of anger at her own foolishness filled her eyes with tears. She turned and slid down the door to sit forlornly on the floor with her arms wrapped around her shins and her chin on her knees.

The night pressed in at the yawning window. There was no way in the world that she dared make the perilous climb to Alex's window. The lip of brickwork wouldn't support her. She'd slip. She'd fall. No way.

Long, agonising minutes ticked timelessly away. Occasionally she heard footsteps from somewhere in the house. Muffled voices. A door closing.

She was mesmerised by the black square of the open window. It was like a gaping mouth waiting to swallow her if she came too close.

'No,' she whispered aloud. 'It's no good. I can't do it.'

Yes. You can. The voice was so clear in her mind that for a split second she thought someone had spoken to her. Her mother.

She stood up. Very slowly. She walked to the window.

Her heart was pounding. Her limbs felt weak. She stretched a leg out through the window. She was aware of a stiffness in her hip. A memory of her injury.

She paused. This was madness. She wasn't fit enough to do this. Her hip would betray her and she'd plunge down on to the stones. She sat on the wide sill, trying to control her rapid breathing. She had never done anything in her life that had scared her so much.

She shifted her weight. The night was cool, but sweat ran down her face and her whole body felt feverishly hot. In her mind, she saw the repeating image of those hard patio stones rushing up to smash her falling body.

She strained down to put her foot on the narrow cornice. She pressed down, clinging to the window frame for safety. The brickwork held.

It was now or it was never.

It was the thought of Alex lying hurt in that locked room that tipped the balance. She slid off the sill and brought her other foot down on to the cornice. She clung to the window sill.

For a few moments, her only thought was to climb straight back into the safety of her room. But she forced her fingers to unlock themselves from the window. She edged her feet – one by one – along the lip of brickwork. Edge, edge.

The worst moment of all came when she reached the end of the window and had to let go of the last remaining handhold. The white plaster wall was smooth and featureless. The next window was two metres away. To carry on, she would have to press herself to the wall and pray that the cornice would hold.

She hugged the wall. It seemed to tip and spin, as though trying to throw her off. She knew that she'd fall. It was inevitable. There was nothing to be done about it.

She had no idea how long she stood there, spread-eagled against the white plaster – frozen by terror. Eventually the panic subsided a little – enough to allow her to shuffle slowly along.

The next window seemed an impossible distance away. Her fingers crawled over the wall, reaching for the edge of the windowframe. Her feet moved a centimetre at a time.

She reached the window. It was not the safe haven she had expected. The sill jutted out, forcing her to bend out into emptiness – and there was nothing to hold on to. She was glad when she was past it. The wall was grazing her hands and cheek. Her hip and leg ached.

This was insanity.

She shouldn't be doing this.

What was the point?

To see Alex.

Yes.

That was the point.

She edged onwards. The second window drew slowly closer. She was almost there. A kind of dangerous euphoria erupted in her mind. She'd done it! She lurched towards the window.

Her foot slipped. The wall slid past her as she fell

sideways, her foot treading suddenly on nothing. She managed to snatch at the sill as she fell. Her fingers gripped the smooth stone. Her arms and shoulders were wrenched as her hands took her full weight. She wasted energy scrabbling frantically at the flat surface of the wall. Her feet could find no purchase. They fell away under her.

She hung in the darkness like a rag doll. Unable to move. Unable to pull herself up.

✷

Danny was becoming frustrated. He'd been squatting in the back of the MSU for over half an hour. He knew no more now than when he had first teased the tracer signal out of all that background noise.

'Come on, you guys! Show me something!' He whacked a device with the flat of his hand. Impact maintenance. Instant remorse. 'Sorry. Sorry.' He stroked the box of wires and electronic chip-boards.

It was maddening. He knew that one of the tracers was in that house. But which one? The one in the envelope of diamonds – or the one on Maddie? The only way to confirm whether Alex and Maddie were in the house was to make contact with Alex. Which was what Danny had been unsuccessfully trying to do for over thirty minutes.

The transmitter and receivers were within range – but the air was full of white noise. It was like trying to listen to a single quiet voice in the middle of a howling mob.

Danny adjusted the headset and bent in on himself, closing his eyes to help with his concentration. His fingers moved assuredly over dials and faders.

'Alex?' he said for the thousandth time. 'Alex? Are you in there?'

The airwaves crackled and roared. He strained to hear a reply.

Nothing.

He leaned back. Angry. He felt like driving his foot through all that useless equipment. Watching it fizz and crackle would be very satisfying. And then a thought struck him.

'Idiot!' he whispered. 'Danny, you stupid brainless idiot!' He reached forwards and began to switch things off and pull wires out of jack sockets. He thought that maybe he had the answer.

The hi-tech electronics were sucking up the white noise – concentrating it – amplifying it. Maybe if everything was turned off, Danny would be able to get some response through his mobile. It had to be worth a try.

●

Alex lay in darkness. His head still ached from the impact of the gun when they were in the helicopter. When he shut his eyes, red flames throbbed and flickered in the blackness behind his lids. The thug had struck him only twice – a fist to his stomach and a swipe across his mouth with the back of his hand. The blows had been meant as a warning. A sample of what he might expect if he didn't behave himself. Alex knew that next time he wouldn't get off so lightly.

A tooth had cut his lip and he could taste blood. His wrists were bound with grey tape. He fingers felt numb. A thin chain had been wound around his ankles and then padlocked to the bed frame. He was relieved that they had not discovered the tiny microphone or the transmitter, but Danny was miles away now – well out of range.

He could sit up – with difficulty. He could roll from one side to the other. Or he could lie there staring up at the ceiling with his head teeming with black thoughts.

His mood was sombre and desperate. He blamed himself for everything that had happened – and everything that was going to happen. He should never have taken Maddie to Heathrow. It had been crazy. Dangerous and brainless and crazy.

But Alex's mind wasn't only occupied with recriminations against himself. The next day would bring a whole new set of problems. Eddie Stone was expected at the house. Bryson had said nothing about it, but the muscleman had let it slip.

'Mr Stone will be here in the morning,' he had said as he'd been tying the chain around Alex's ankles. 'You'd better behave yourself.' He had paused for a moment, snapping the padlock shut. He had looked into Alex's face. 'Mr Stone's not as sweet-tempered as I am.'

So far as Alex could tell, Bryson and the woman still believed that they had captured Henry Dean and Grace O'Connor. That's what they would tell Eddie Stone when he arrived. There was no reason for Stone to believe otherwise. But their disguises wouldn't hold for long. Stone would want to make contact with Patrick O'Connor. He'd want to let the American businessman know that his daughter was in their hands. Then things would start to get unpleasant.

O'Connor would demand proof that they really did have Grace. A digital photo, maybe, emailed to him. Her voice over the telephone. Something totally convincing.

Maddie would be unmasked.

Then what would happen?

Eddie Stone would want to know who their two prisoners really were – and he'd want to know quickly. Alex's blood ran cold at the thought of what methods Stone might employ to get the truth out of them.

And what if he learned who Maddie was? How would Michael Stone's son react when he discovered that Bryson was holding Jack Cooper's daughter prisoner?

Alex writhed uselessly in his bonds – indifferent to the pain of the chain biting into his ankles – fighting ineffectually to prise his wrists apart.

A sudden noise from outside his window made him freeze. A strange sound. Close by. A scraping, slithering sound – as if there was something or someone out there.

He struggled to sit up, staring at the black curtain.

He thought he heard a gasp – or it might have been a gust of air.

There was a brief scratching sound, like something scrabbling against the wall. Then there was silence again.

He listened intently for a few moments.

No. Nothing.

And then he heard another sound.

The sound of wood scraping on wood.

Someone was trying to force the window open.

Chapter Fifteen

Maddie had come through too much to fail now. The shooting. The loss of her mother. Months of pain and despair. And then rekindled hope and purpose with PIC. She wasn't going to let it all end in a fall in the night on to cold, hard stone.

She was running now on willpower alone. Somehow she managed to find the strength in her arms to gradually pull herself up. It was agonising. She got a knee on to the cornice. An elbow over the windowsill. She rested for a few moments, pumping air into her lungs, her head spinning.

She pulled herself up so that she was standing on the cornice again. Relatively safe. The sill pressed against her, as if trying to push her off. The glass was cold against her palms.

If the window was locked, she had risked all this for nothing. She pressed her fingers up against the sash. She pushed upwards. The window grated open a few centimetres.

The relief was breathtaking. She slid her fingers in under the sash and heaved upwards. Curtains billowed. She tipped forwards and let herself fall into the darkened room.

'Maddie?' Alex's voice was a harsh whisper in the gloom.

'Yes. Yes,' Maddie panted. She untangled herself from the trailing curtains and managed to stand up. Her legs felt watery. She saw Alex sitting up on the bed. She tottered forwards. 'I climbed across... ' she gasped, 'there was a ledge... I nearly fell... '

'Are you all right?' Alex asked urgently. 'Have they hurt you?'

'No. How about you?'

'I've been better. Maddie – listen to me – you've got to get out of here. If they find out who you really are—'

'I'm not leaving without you.' She knelt on the bed. 'We'll get out together.' She began to unpeel the tape from around his wrists. A savage, defiant grin appeared briefly. 'I'm rescuing you,' she said as she unwound the tape. 'We'll find a way out. Somehow.'

Alex rubbed his numbed hands together and the blood began to flow again. He leaned forwards, trying to examine in the darkness the chain that bound his ankles.

'I need some light,' she said. 'I can't see what I'm doing.'

'No,' Alex said. 'No light. It might be seen.'

Maddie felt the heavy padlock. 'I can't open this,' she said. 'We need something to cut the chain with.'

'I left my boltcutters in my other suit,' Alex said.

Maddie looked at him. 'I don't know how to get you loose.' She stared around the darkened room, as if she hoped to find some sharp cutting edge lying nearby.

'Listen, Maddie,' Alex began. 'Forget about that. I want you to—' He stopped. A faint voice had sounded suddenly in his ear.

'Alex? Are you there? Alex? *Be* there, dammit!'

'Danny?'

'Alex!' There was a wild whoop of joy through the tiny earpiece. 'Oh, ma-an! You have no idea how long I've been trying to get through to you. What the hell is going on in there, Alex? Is Maddie with you?'

Maddie was staring at Alex. Immobile. Hardly daring to believe.

Alex looked at her. 'Yes, she's right here. She's fine. We're both fine.'

'When you flew off in that chopper,' Danny said excitedly, 'I thought I'd never see you guys again. I was thinking – how am I gonna explain this to the DCS? You guys scared the life out of me!'

'Listen, Danny,' Alex said. 'They've got us locked up. I don't know what they plan to do with us, but—'

'I do!' Maddie interrupted. 'I know exactly what they're planning.'

It didn't take long for Maddie to fill Danny and Alex in on everything she had been told.

'There's more,' Alex said. 'They're expecting Eddie Stone sometime in the morning.'

'Oops!' said Danny.

'Oops is right,' said Alex.

'He's gonna get straight on to Pat O'Connor.'

'Right!'

'O'Connor will say – hey, that's not my daughter.'

'I'm way ahead of you, Danny.' Alex looked at Maddie. She was only hearing half of this. 'You have to get us out of here before Stone arrives.'

'OK,' Danny said. 'Here's what's going to happen. I want you guys to sit tight while Uncle Danny does all the hard work. I'll have you safe and sound before you know it. That's a promise.'

'No!' Maddie said to Alex when he had conveyed this message to her. 'Tell him he has to wait.'

'Danny?' Alex said. 'Maddie says to wait.' He looked at her. 'Why wait?'

'This is our best chance of linking everything together,' Maddie said urgently. 'You said Stone is coming here in the morning. If Danny calls in a task force to release us, he won't come.'

'But we'll still have Bryson,' Alex said. 'Bryson is a direct link to Stone.'

Maddie shook her head. 'Stone could deny that he knew anything about this. We could lose our best chance of nailing him.' Her voice was insistent. 'Stone *has* to come here – and he won't come if the place is swarming with police.'

'She's crazy, Alex,' Danny said into the earpiece. 'Tell her she's crazy.'

'Danny doesn't think it's a good idea,' Alex said to Maddie. 'I'm with him. We need to get you out. Forget Stone. He can wait. It's too risky.'

Maddie's eyes blazed. 'We have to risk it,' she said

adamantly. 'Michael Stone had my mother and father gunned down in the street.' She shivered. 'For all we know, the man who did it could be in this house. If we can just hold things together until Eddie Stone gets here, we might be able to take them all out in one hit.'

Alex relayed this to Danny. 'This house isn't on our Stonecor file,' he added. 'This could be the place where all the dodgy stuff is kept. If we can actually pick Eddie Stone up while he's on the premises, he could wind up sharing a cell with his dad.'

'Yeah – or the two of you could wind up at the bottom of the Thames with cement boots on your feet,' Danny said.

Alex didn't pass this on to Maddie. He looked at her. Weighing her up. She had held things together amazingly well so far. If Stonecor was shut down for good, it would give her some kind of closure on all the horrors of the past year.

Alex hesitated. His decisions so far had not been good.

Their eyes met in the gloom. Maddie's gaze was uncompromising.

'Danny?' Alex said. 'Stay close by. Get through to Control and fill them in on the situation. Tell them we need a task force over here on standby, but that they're to keep a low profile until I give the word.'

Maddie smiled grimly and nodded.

'And, Danny?' Alex added. 'When I do give the word, I want this place locked down as fast as possible, got me?'

'Gotcha!' Danny said. 'I'll be in touch. Tell Maddie to be careful.'

'Will do.'

The line was cut.

Alex looked at Maddie in silence for a few moments. 'Can you do this?' he asked.

She nodded.

'Danny thinks you're crazy.'

'He's probably right.'

Alex held his arms out, wrists together. 'You'd better tie me up again,' he said.

Reluctantly, Maddie began to wind the tape back around Alex's wrists.

'And you'll have to go out the same way you came,' Alex said.

Maddie swallowed hard. 'Yes,' she said. 'I'm trying not to think about it.'

✷

The only way Danny had managed to filter out all the electronic white noise and get an audible fix on Alex was to shut down virtually everything in the MSU. It had worked, although the signal had been weak. Now, as Danny crouched wearily under the dim roof light, he discovered he had a new problem.

A small panel on his mobile showed low battery. It wasn't critical yet, but if he wasn't careful, the time would soon come when he could no longer keep in contact with Alex.

He frowned. 'Why the heck didn't you include a mobile phone charger with all this junk?' he asked himself aloud, staring around the van. 'Are you stupid, Danny, or what?'

He switched on the transmitter and slid the fader to a new frequency. The device hissed at him. Whatever gear it was that they had in that house, it was causing havoc in the MSU. Danny tried boosting the output and dampening the interference. His efforts were met with a howl that went through his head like a knife.

He switched it off again.

'The way I see it, Danny,' he muttered. 'You have two choices, here. Either you use your mobile, or you go look for a public phone.' He didn't like the idea of leaving the van. He had parked in clear view of the side windows of the house. With two prisoners on the premises, the people inside were hardly likely to have all tucked themselves up for the night. Someone would be on guard in there. And if that someone happened to look out of the window and see Danny climbing out of the van – then that someone might get suspicious.

No. It was better to risk draining the mobile a little. He pressed for Control.

It only rang twice before a female voice responded.

'Special Branch emergency line, how may I help you?'

Danny was puzzled. Special Branch? How had he come through to Special Branch? 'I want to get through to Police Investigation Command,' Danny said. 'It's urgent.'

'I'm afraid there's no one available,' the woman said. 'Direct lines to Police Investigation Command will re-open at six thirty in the morning. How may I help you?'

Of course! PIC Control didn't have twenty-four-hour coverage. At night, all calls were routed through Special Branch. Danny's brain raced. If he involved Special Branch at this stage, they would take over. They'd use their own protocols. They'd probably storm the place. They certainly wouldn't be interested in the opinions of two PIC trainees and a sixteen-year-old on work experience.

Danny knew how badly it would reflect on PIC if he

called in Special Branch. This whole disaster would come out. It would look like Jack Cooper's trainees were out of control. Questions would be asked about the involvement of Cooper's daughter. That could have bad repercussions for Jack Cooper and the whole department.

Danny gnawed his thumbnail. *Dammit!*

'How may I help you?' asked the voice for a third time.

'Direct lines to PIC re-open at six-thirty, right?' he asked.

'That's correct.'

'Fine!' Danny had made his decision. 'Thanks.' He cut the line. Unless something catastrophic happened, things should stay calm in the house through the rest of the night. At 6:30 precisely, he would call PIC Control and have them patch him through to Kevin Randal or Roland Jakes or one of the other unit commanders. There would still be time to assemble an effective taskforce at the house before things started to get busy.

Danny stared at his low-battery warning display.

He hoped he'd made the right decision.

Maddie and Alex's lives might depend on it.

✪

Maddie lay on her bed. She was shaking all over. Feverish. She had just been sick. The terror had finally got to her. The climb back had been the stuff of nightmares. She had hoped it might be easier the second time around – but, if anything, it had been worse. Her hands were still trembling from the effort. Her tights were holed from the grazing of her legs along the wall. The dress was torn.

But worse than all of that were the hideous memories that swarmed around her head as she lay there in the darkness of that prison room. The memory of a hail of bullets in the night. Of pain and anguish and shock. Of blood on the pavement. Of that mocking voice. *Goodnight – from Mr Stone.*

Michael Stone had arranged for the shooting. It couldn't be proven in a court of law – but it was true all the same. But Michael Stone hadn't actually pulled the trigger. Someone else had done that. A hired killer. A man such as Richard Bryson. Or that big brute who had hit Alex.

The thought that she could be under the same roof as the man who had murdered her mother and crippled her father sent another wave of nausea through Maddie's aching body. She stumbled to the bathroom and was sick again.

She looked at her face in the mirror. She was haggard. Ashen.

'I can't do this,' she whispered. 'It's not possible. I just want to go home.' Her head hung as tears ran down her face. 'I don't want this to be happening!' For five minutes she wept in weakness and despair.

Then, a kind of calmness came over her. She lifted her head again and stared into her reflected eyes. She felt oddly blank. Drained. She washed her face.

She threw herself on to the bed. She was so tired. She wasn't going to be able to sleep. No way. But she was exhausted. Worn away to aching fragments.

She closed her eyes.

Her body felt leaden.

She felt as if she was falling down into a great dark pit.

She lay strewn on the bed like a survivor washed up from a shipwreck.

Sleep came down over her like a hideous monster, unquiet and filled with horrible, vivid nightmares.

Chapter Sixteen

06:00 a.m.

Richard Bryson was awake early. Prowling the corridors. Eager for Eddie Stone's arrival. He had slept well. This was going to be his day. Things hadn't been good for him in Stonecor since Eddie had taken over. There wasn't the same level of loyalty and trust any more – not like when Eddie's father had been running the business. Richard felt that he had been sidelined. Today, all that would change.

Richard Bryson would be back on top. Snatching the girl would tip the balance in the negotiations with O'Connor. The cocky American would be in the palm of their hand. Things would be sweet. All thanks to him.

It was early still, but Eddie could arrive at any time. It was best to have everything ready. Bryson walked slowly up the stairs. Smiling to himself.

He unlocked the door to Alex's room. Darkness. Silence. He walked across to the bed. Henry Dean seemed to be asleep. Bryson leaned over him. Alex's shirtfront had got twisted. A button had come open.

Bryson reached out to shake his prisoner awake. Then something caught his eye. He grabbed the disarrayed shirtfront and ripped it open. Alex woke with a start.

'What the hell—' Bryson tore the wire from Alex's chest. The tiny transmitter dangled from his fist, turning slowly. He bounded to the window and wrenched the curtains open. The early morning light confirmed what he already knew. Henry Dean was wired for sound!

Alex was watching him from the bed. Wide awake. Alarmed. Ready for the worst.

Bryson turned and walked towards him. 'What's this?'

Alex looked at him. 'You know what it is.'

'What's the game, Henry?' Bryson let the transmitter rest on his open palm. 'This can't have a range of more than a few hundred metres. Who are you in contact with?'

'No one,' Alex said.

'Is there someone out there? Someone you've been talking to?' Richard loped to the window and stared out over the gardens. He angled his head. Beyond the trees and the wall, the street was lined with cars.

He hammered his fist against the window frame. 'Right! Let's get this sorted.' He ran to the door, flicking a finger towards Alex. 'I'll deal with you later.'

Alex heard him shouting. 'Jack! I want you outside. Search the whole area.' There was the clatter of his feet on the stairs and his voice moved out of hearing, still barking orders. Not that Alex had to hear him to know what was going on. Bryson was sending the thug out into the street to find Danny.

Things had just got a whole lot worse.

✪

A neon-lit night. Mum on one side. Dad on the other. Out through a doorway and into the street. A hooded figure. Gunshots. Blazing pain. A fall into darkness.

A recurring dream.

Maddie felt the grip of a hand on her shoulder. Shaking her.

She awoke with a stifled yell. She was disorientated for a few moments. An unfamiliar face bent over her.

The horrible dream crashed headlong into an equally unpleasant reality.

'Grace! Wake up! Now!' It was Celia. Her voice was urgent.

Maddie ran her hands over her face, trying to force her blurry eyes to focus.

She stared up at the woman.

'I need you awake and alert,' Celia said. There was an edge to her voice that Maddie hadn't heard before. 'Get up and get dressed, please.'

Maddie could hardly remember getting out of her clothes the previous night. Somehow she had found the energy to peel off the torn dress – somewhere between midnight and dawn. She had opened Grace's suitcase and had found a T-shirt to wear in bed.

'What's happened?' Maddie asked, still struggling to get a grip on the day.

'How well do you know Henry?' Celia asked her.

Sleep fell away from Maddie in an instant. 'What's happened to him?'

'Nothing's happened to him,' Celia said. She drew back the bedcovers. 'If you and Henry are in this together, you'd be well advised to tell me everything right now. There's no point lying to us. We already know all about Henry. He's told us everything.' Her hand grasped Maddie's wrist. 'You may as well tell me the whole story. I promise no harm will come to you – or to him. You have my word on that.'

Maddie's brain was whirling. What was going on here? What had they found out? If they really knew the truth, why was Celia still referring to Alex as Henry?

'I don't know what you're talking about,' Maddie said, pulling her arm out of Celia's grip. 'What's Henry done?'

'Give it up, Grace,' Celia said. 'We found the wire.'

Maddie's pretence of shock and surprise was spot-on. 'What do you mean, *wire*?' She *was* shocked – and scared – but she had to fake ignorance, too.

'Henry was carrying a short-range transmitter,' Celia said. Her eyes hardened. 'Who was he talking to, Grace? For your own sake – tell me everything before Mr Bryson gets here.' Her voice lowered to a sinister hiss. 'He won't be as polite as me, Grace. Trust me. He'll set Jack Clay on you.'

Maddie gave her a cold stare. 'Why are you asking me who he was talking to?' she said. 'You said Henry had told you everything.' She knew she had to play this perfectly. One wrong word now and all hell could break loose.

'We just need you to confirm his story, Grace,' Celia

said. Her voice was calmer now. 'Just tell me the truth, please.'

Maddie sat up. 'The truth is that I don't know what you're talking about,' she said icily. 'And now, I'd be really grateful if you'd leave, so I can wash and put some clothes on.' She got out of bed and stood there, staring defiantly into Celia's eyes. 'Is that OK?'

The door opened. Bryson was standing there.

Celia looked at him. 'Sorry, Mr Bryson,' she said. 'I did my best.'

Bryson nodded. He looked at Maddie. 'Pity,' he said. 'Now I'm going to have to ask your boyfriend some difficult questions.' He smiled. 'You understand what I mean by difficult, don't you Grace? Difficult for him – not for me.'

Maddie was afraid that she understood Bryson only too well. He was going to try to force the truth out of Alex.

'Of course, you could still save him from a very unpleasant interview,' Bryson said smoothly. 'Do you want to do that, Grace? Do you want to tell me why Henry was carrying a wire – who he was in communication with?'

A door slammed downstairs before Maddie could

respond. The front door. Heavy footsteps echoed. A deep voice called up.

'Mr Bryson?' It was Jack Clay. 'I found it! It was a white van – parked across the street.'

A smile spread across Richard Bryson's face. 'Excellent!' he said to Maddie. 'It looks like I won't be needing your help after all, Grace.' He turned and disappeared.

Maddie reeled from the dreadful news.

They had found Danny.

Now all three of them were at the mercy of Richard Bryson.

✪

It was 06:23

The back doors of the MSU hung ajar. There were scrape marks and gouges near the handle – showing where a jemmy had been used to get the van open. The delicate electronic equipment inside had been trashed. Jack Clay had destroyed everything. Wires and cables trailed across the floor of the van. Instrument panels were buckled and wrecked – strewn about – overturned.

On the floor, near the back doors, Danny's mobile lay in pieces. A heavy heel had cracked down on it – smashing it beyond repair – just like everything else.

Chapter Seventeen

'Hungry, are you?' There was a smile on the shopkeeper's face as he loaded the bag.

'A guy's gotta eat,' said Danny. He scooped up a pack of M&Ms and slid them across the counter. They were followed by two Mars bars, a chunky Kit Kat, and a tube of Pringles.

Danny wasn't hungry. He was ravenous. 'You open early,' he said.

'It's the newspapers,' the shopkeeper explained. 'They arrive at 5:30.'

'Bummer!' Danny handed over the money. He was already eating one of the pre-packed sandwiches as he left the shop.

Hunger and thirst had driven him from the MSU. It had been sheer luck that he had found an open cornershop within a couple of hundred yards.

He flipped open a yoghurt drink and downed it in one long swig.

He looked at his watch.

It was almost 6:30. Nearly time to put that call through to PIC Control. The troops would arrive. Maddie and Alex would be rescued. The panic would be over – bar the inevitable debriefing with Jack Cooper.

Danny wasn't looking forward to that. He could almost hear Cooper's acid voice. *You decided to run a mission on your own – and you thought it would be a good idea to involve my daughter? Would you like to explain your thought processes to me before or after I throw the book at you?*

Yowch! That was going to be bad.

As he approached Addison Road, Danny became cautious again. People might be up and about in the big house. He didn't want to walk straight into a trap.

He tore the M&Ms bag open with his teeth.

He peered around the corner.

'Damn!'

The coloured M&Ms cascaded to the pavement and rolled underfoot.

The back doors of the van were gaping.

The inside of the van looked like someone had been at it with a sledgehammer. It was a mess.

A shiver ran through him.

If he hadn't slipped out to get some food – he would have been part of that mess.

He reached for his mobile.

'Oh, no!' It wasn't at his belt. He had left it in the van.

But then a worse thought hit him. Why had they come looking for the van? They must have found something. The tracer. Or Alex's wire. Either way, Alex and Maddie were toast, unless he could do something quickly.

But what? He couldn't just march up to the front door and demand to be let in.

He backed away, his heart thumping.

They needed him. And they needed him *now*.

He had to get into the house. But how?

A van came cruising along the road – bright red and with the Royal Mail logo on its side. It was like the answer to a prayer.

Danny's eyes widened and a grin spread across his face.

A Royal Mail delivery van! Yesss!

He dropped the bag of food. Hunger and thirst were forgotten in the adrenaline rush of action.

He stepped into the road and lifted a hand to stop the van.

The driver gestured for him to move.

Danny stood firm.

The van came to an abrupt halt ten centimetres from Danny's legs.

He moved around to the driver's window.

'Are you some kind of nut?' the driver asked. 'You're going to get yourself killed, pulling stunts like that.'

'That wouldn't surprise me in the least,' Danny said, reaching for his ID card. 'But right now – if you'd bear with me for a moment or two – I could really use your help.'

✪

Alex was in a room that had been transformed into an office. The furnishings were spare – black, silver, white wood. The bare floorboards had been bleached white. A long work unit was filled with banks of electronic equipment. Computers hummed on screensaver. Locked filing cabinets lined one entire wall.

Alex was sitting in a revolving chair. Loops of grey tape bound him securely to it – wrists and chest. His ankles were also wrapped in the tape.

Bryson was sitting on a desk, his feet up on another chair. He was watching Alex with hooded, predatory eyes. Clay stood by the door – a big, blunt lump of menace. His eyes were blank. Switched off. Waiting for instructions.

'There are two ways of approaching this problem,' Bryson said to Alex, his voice soft and slow. 'There's the direct route – where you tell me what I want to know right now. Or there's the scenic route – where I let Jack loose on you for a while – and *then* you tell me what I want to know.' He smiled. 'Either way is OK by me. It's your choice.'

Alex hadn't been given much time to think. Events were speeding up around him. He knew the MSU had been found – but there had been no mention of Danny. Possibly, he was still free. Possibly, help was coming.

Stall for time. That was all he could do.

'I was given the wire by Mr O'Connor,' Alex said.

Bryson frowned. 'You'll have to explain that a bit more thoroughly, Henry.' He took a slender silver file out of an inner pocket of his jacket and began to clean his already scrupulously clean nails. His head was bowed, his eyes concentrating on his hands. 'Start explaining just as soon as you're ready,' he said. 'I'll give you three seconds – then I'll ask Mr Clay to twist your head off and kick it around the room for a while.'

Alex shivered at the mildness of Bryson's voice. It made the threat all the more chilling.

'This whole business was set up by Mr O'Connor,' Alex said. 'He arranged for me to contact you – for Grace and I to fly over here with the diamonds.' He raised his voice. 'It was a test, Richard. Mr O'Connor was testing you people out – and you failed big time.'

'How so?' Bryson asked gently.

'When Mr O'Connor is planning on taking on new business partners, he likes to know everything there is to know about them. He likes to get under their skin – to find out how they tick. I've been in constant contact with Mr O'Connor – he knows exactly what's been going on. And he doesn't like it, Richard. He really doesn't like it when people mess with his family.'

Bryson's head lifted. There was suspicion and doubt in his eyes. 'He used his daughter as bait?'

'I guess you could put it like that.'

A muscle twitched under Richard Bryson's right eye. It was the only sign of the sudden unease that Alex's words had created in him.

The door opened. Celia leaned in. 'Sorry to disturb you, Mr Bryson,' she said. 'But I've just heard from Mr Stone – he'll be here in about five minutes.'

Bryson didn't respond. Celia stared at him for a few moments, then withdrew, quietly closing the door behind herself.

'Mr Bryson?' Jack Clay's voice was a seismic growl. 'What do you want me to do?'

Bryson flashed him a look. 'I want you to beat the truth out of our friend here,' he said. 'He's lying to us. There's no way O'Connor would use his daughter as live bait. There's something else going on here – and I want to know what it is.'

'Patrick O'Connor is going to squash you like a bug,' Alex said to Bryson. He looked at Clay. 'Richard has blown it,' he said. 'Use your brain, Jack – get on the winning team.'

Stall. Delay. Pray for help.

A faint, rhythmic beating sound filtered into the room.

Richard Bryson slid down off the desk and walked to the window.

A distant black dot grew in the pale blue sky.

A helicopter. Coming in from the east.

Richard turned to Alex. He pointed a finger. 'Do

you know what?' he said. 'It doesn't matter whether O'Connor set this up or not. Either way, we win. We've got his daughter.' His face hardened. 'And if your boss doesn't play ball with us, he's going to get her back in bite-sized pieces!'

He stalked across the room and slammed out.

Alex looked at Jack Clay.

The hefty man was staring out of the window at the approaching helicopter, like a big dog anticipating its master's return.

✪

Maddie was locked in. She was certain that Alex was suffering at the hands of Bryson and the brutal Clay – but there was nothing she could do about it. She dreaded footsteps outside her room. The unlocking of the door. A horrible smile on Bryson's face – a smile that would mean that the truth had finally been beaten out of Alex.

And then what?

A noise drew Maddie to the window. A far-away chugging sound. An engine. Rotorblades cutting the air.

The helicopter hung like a black teardrop in the clear sky. The aircraft moved swiftly closer to the house. Treetops thrashed. It hovered above the

garden. It began to descend. The engine roared. The foliage was forced back by the beat of the blades. The grass lay flat. The windows rattled.

Eddie Stone was coming home.

Maddie's hands pressed flat against the glass, her fingers spread wide. Her breath misted the pane. Her heart was pounding.

The helicopter settled and the engine was cut.

Gradually the blur of the blades began to slow.

A door opened in the black machine. A man stepped out. He was tall and slim. He wore a long black coat. He carried a black briefcase. He was speaking into a mobile. His dark hair was whipped by the wind. He didn't duck away from the whipping blades. He strode across the lawn.

Eddie Stone.

Maddie watched him from her high window. He was young. Good-looking. Successful. Confident. Maddie bit her lip. His father had ordered the assassination of *her* family.

It felt weird to be watching him like that. Eerie. Scary.

A familiar figure came across from the house to meet him. Richard Bryson.

The two men spoke briefly. Even without sound and

from such a distance, it was clear who had the authority.

Moments after the encounter, Eddie Stone brushed past Bryson and moved out of sight into the house.

Maddie turned. She felt weak. She leaned against the window. Watching the door. Waiting. Frozen.

Frozen like a small animal on a motorway as the deadly headlights rush towards it.

Waiting for her nightmare to become reality.

Chapter Eighteen

Eddie Stone swept into the office. Richard Bryson was at his heels.

Eddie took in the scene at a glance. Jack Clay standing by the window. The man bound to the chair. A stranger. Young. Good-looking. Powerfully built. Angry and wary.

'Mr Stone.' Clay's voice was a low growl.

'Jack.' Eddie Stone gave him a nod. He turned slowly, his piercing blue eyes raking over Richard Bryson's face. 'Who's this?'

Bryson forced a smile. 'He's the surprise I just told you about,' he said. 'Him and the girl.' He paused, licking his lips. 'I've been hard at work, Eddie. You'll be impressed.'

'I'll be the judge of that,' Eddie Stone said coldly. 'What exactly have you been doing? Make it quick, Richard. I've got work to do. Just tell me why there's some guy taped to a chair in my office, giving me the evil eye. Are you crazy – bringing people here? What on earth have you been up to?'

Bryson moved around Eddie Stone. 'His name is Henry Dean – but *he's* not the real surprise, Eddie. His girlfriend is the real surprise. His girlfriend is called Grace.'

Eddie Stone stared at Bryson. He reached out a long slim arm and gripped Bryson's shoulder. Bryson winced. 'Speak some sense to me, Richard. I've had a heavy night. I don't have time for guessing games.'

'I've snatched Grace O'Connor,' Bryson said. 'She's here. Right now. She's upstairs. O'Connor will have to agree to our terms now.' His face was eager. 'I've won the deal for you, Eddie. We're going to get everything we wanted.'

Eddie Stone's face went white. 'This is a joke,' he said softly. 'Tell me this is a joke, Richard.'

Bryson's smile wavered. 'No,' he said. 'It's true. What happened was—'

Eddie Stone's fingers gnawed into Bryson's shoulder. His voice was a sinister hiss. 'I've just come

177

from a ten-hour session with Patrick O'Connor's negotiating team, Richard,' he whispered. 'We worked right through the night. We've got the whole deal sewn up.' His voice rose. 'Everyone is happy, Richard. Everything is perfect. I've just come off the phone with Pat O'Connor himself. Do you know what his final words to me were, Richard? He said, "I'm glad I've finally met a man I can do business with." '

He lifted his other hand and slowly patted Richard Bryson's cheek in time to his words. 'You stupid, meddling, moronic clown, Richard. If this wrecks my deal with O'Connor, you have my promise that I will kill you. Personally.' The blood drained from Bryson's face. The look in Eddie Stone's eyes terrified him.

Eddie Stone released him. He looked at Jack Clay and pointed at Alex. 'Cut him loose.' He walked to the open doorway. He paused, looking at Bryson over his shoulder. 'Where is she?'

'Second floor. Third bedroom.'

Eddie Stone reached out his arm, his fingers curled into claws. 'You're out of the business, Richard. You're finished! Jack – watch him – keep him here – I haven't done with him yet.'

He closed the door. He paused for a moment or two. His eyes shut. Leaning one hand against the wall.

Breathing deeply. Controlling himself. Calmness over fury. He could still rescue the situation if he kept his head. Richard would probably have to be dealt with very harshly to keep O'Connor sweet – but that would be a small price to pay. The man was worse than useless.

Eddie Stone bounded up the long staircase, his long coat billowing out behind him. He just hoped Grace O'Connor was the forgiving kind.

✪

Richard Bryson wasn't a fool. He had seen his future in Eddie Stone's bleak, ice-blue eyes. No future.

Jack Clay was stripping the tape away from Alex's wrists.

Alex had no idea where this turn of events would lead – but at least he would be free to make a difference now. Clay was huge – but size wasn't everything. Alex knew techniques that could drop him like a stone.

Jack Clay stooped to unwind the tape from around his ankles. Over his bent back, Alex saw Bryson move swiftly to the desk. The black briefcase lay on it. Alex remembered the gun. Bryson snapped the briefcase lock open. He lifted the lid. Alex saw the desperation in his face.

Richard Bryson had no future. Unless he could get himself out of here before Jack Clay moved in on him. That was his only hope of survival.

He drew the gun from its black silk covering. He pointed it at Jack Clay's back. His hand was trembling.

Alex watched him – tensed and poised. He was almost free. He was almost ready to act. Another couple of loops of the tape, and Clay would get both feet in the face. Then Alex would only have to deal with Bryson and the gun. Only.

The doorbell rang. A sharp, bright chime.

Jack Clay stood up and looked towards the door. He hadn't even noticed that Bryson was pointing the gun at him.

In the eerie silence, they all heard the sharp click of heels out in the hall as Celia Thomson went to answer the door

It was 06:50.

The house in Addison Road had an early caller.

✪

06:47

A bright red Royal Mail van came cruising around the corner of Addison Road and moved into the side street. It came to a stop outside the large white corner house. The driver picked up a clipboard. He yanked the door back and stepped down into the road. He glanced up at the house – at all those staring windows. He adjusted his blue uniform jacket and walked quickly up the stone steps to the front door of the house.

He rang the bell.

He heard the click-click of approaching women's shoes from within.

The door was opened by an attractive, smartly dressed woman.

'Special delivery,' said the postman. 'I need a signature.' He gave the woman a wide smile. 'Looks like it'll be a nice day.' It was what the Brits did – they were always talking about the weather. Danny knew that.

The woman cut him with a brief, razor-blade smile. She had been in the kitchen at the back of the house – fixing breakfast for her boss.

'Give it to me, then,' she said, reaching for the clipboard.

'Uh – the package is for a Mr E. Stone,' Danny said. 'I need him to sign for it.'

'I'm Mr Stone's personal assistant,' the woman said. 'I always sign for him.'

Danny withheld the clipboard. 'Sorry. It says Mr Stone has to sign for it himself.' Danny smiled again.

'This is my first day. I have to do it right. Hey – I'll tell you what – if you can prove who you are – a driver's licence or something like that – I'll let you sign for him. How's that?'

'This is ridiculous,' said Celia Thomson. 'I've never had this problem before.'

'I'm just doing my job,' Danny said. 'Sorry.'

Celia Thomson gave him an exasperated look. 'Wait here.' She turned and clicked her way back across the hall. Danny slipped in and followed her.

She turned, hearing him.

'I told you to—'

Danny lunged at her.

The Plan.

A hand over her mouth. Her arms pinned to her side. Push her in through a handy doorway. Lock her in. Go find Alex and Maddie.

Reality.

She bit his hand and pummelled him with her fists, driving him away. She lashed out with her foot – catching his shin, making him take a stumbling step backwards. He fell. She kicked him again and ran across the hallway towards another door. Shouting for help. Danny grabbed at her legs.

She tripped, twisting as she tumbled. The side of

her head clipped a low table. Her shouts stopped abruptly. Danny scrambled to his feet. Celia Thomson lay sprawled face down on the floor. Very still. He crouched and quickly checked her out. She was out of it. But not badly hurt. She'd wake up with a fine headache.

Danny's eyes narrowed as he stood up. Her yells must have gone right through the house. He listened intently. Waiting to see what would happen next.

He wasn't kept waiting long.

The door towards which the woman had been running flew open.

A man stood there. Filling the doorway. Big as a buffalo.

Small, savage eyes fixed on Danny.

The man moved forwards.

Danny backed off. He came to the far wall of the hallway. He crouched in a martial arts pose – locking eyes with the big man. Trying to seem dangerous.

Jack Clay smiled and shook his head.

Three seconds later, Clay came down on Danny like an avalanche.

☻

Celia Thomson's shouts had rung through the house like a fire alarm. Jack Clay had looked around. He had

unbent his back. His forehead had creased. His hands had closed into fists. He had lumbered towards the door.

Bryson had just stood there. Startled. Confused. His gun pointing at nothing. His other hand gripping the lid of the briefcase. Knuckles white.

Only Alex had an inkling of what might be happening out there. At last. A PIC snatch squad come to rescue them. He had expected something more subtle – but a full-frontal assault was better than nothing.

Alex's eyes darted towards the ceiling. Maddie was up there, locked in a room on the second floor – alone. Or worse – with Eddie Stone. What would Stone do when he heard the noise?

Alex sprang out of the chair – ignoring the aching of his limbs. He dived across the desk at Richard Bryson.

Bryson bounded back, his eyes fierce and deadly. He pointed the gun and fired.

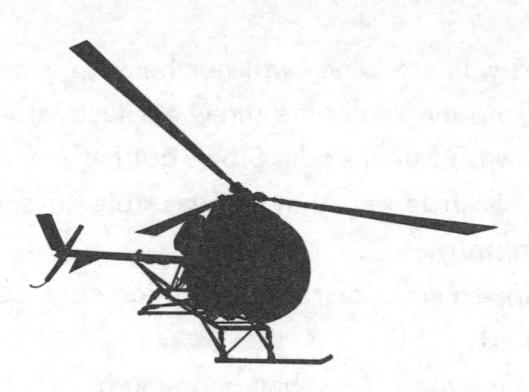

Chapter Nineteen

Maddie heard the click of the key turning in the lock. She stood with her back to the window. Frightened and desperate. Ready to fight for her life.

Eddie Stone stepped into the room.

Maddie's breath hissed.

He moved towards her, his arms spread, his hands open. Conciliatory.

'Grace,' he began. There was an apologetic smile on his face. 'What can I say? This was none of my doing. Bryson acted without consulting me. I can't even begin to apologise properly for what's happened to you.' He put a hand to his forehead. 'The man's gone haywire, Grace. He'll be dealt with, don't you worry.'

Maddie was standing with her back to the light. The bright morning sunshine threw her face into deep shadow. It wasn't until Eddie Stone got halfway across the room towards her, that he was able to see her features properly.

He stopped in mid-stride – in mid-sentence. His eyes widened.

Maddie frowned. What had happened?

A look of recognition spread slowly across Eddie Stone's face.

'Madeleine Cooper.' His voice was a whisper. 'My God! Madeleine Cooper!' He stared at her. 'What on earth has that fool Bryson done?'

Maddie tried to make her voice sound steady. 'Eddie Stone, I am arresting you for kidnapping,' she said. 'This whole house is surrounded by police officers.'

Eddie Stone leaped towards her. Maddie braced herself, lifting her arms in defence. But Stone wasn't interested in her. He pushed her aside and stared out of the window.

'You can't get away,' Maddie said.

'Bryson – you moron – what have you done to me?' Eddie Stone's eyes glittered like ice as he searched for some sign of the heavy police presence of which

Maddie had warned him. The helicopter was standing out on the lawn, the still rotors drooping. The pilot was leaning against the fuselage. Unconcerned. Smoking. At ease.

It was all wrong. Where were the police?

A woman's frantic shouts echoed from downstairs. Eddie Stone spun away from the window.

He snatched Maddie's wrist as he ran for the door. Wincing, Maddie was towed in his wake.

No matter what peril Bryson's stupidity had put him in, Eddie Stone wasn't going down without a fight. If the police were coming for him – they'd have to get to him through Jack Cooper's daughter.

Then came the single shot from Richard Bryson's gun.

✪

'You took your time.' Alex stood in the doorway. Out in the hall, Jack Clay lay stretched on his face like a fallen tree. Danny was massaging his aching hand. He looked up.

'I got here as quick as I could,' he said. 'Why didn't anyone tell me how much it hurts when you karate chop a guy for real? I could have broken my hand.' His eyes were anxious. 'I heard a shot.'

'He missed,' Alex said. 'I've dealt with him.'

'Where's Maddie?'

'Upstairs,' Alex said. 'Stone is up there, too.'

'Then let's go.'

'Wait!' Alex ran back into the office. Danny followed him in. Richard Bryson lay curled in a corner. Unconscious. His gun lay on the floor. Alex crouched and picked the weapon up. He released the bullet clip and dropped it down behind a filing cabinet.

'How do you do that to someone holding a gun?' Danny asked, looking down at Bryson.

'You have to practise a lot,' Alex said.

Danny stared around at the electronics in the room. 'These are the gizmos that were ruining my transmissions,' he said. 'This stuff is amazing.'

'I think this is the safe house where they keep everything that they don't want anyone to know about,' Alex said. 'I wish we had time to go through those filing cabinets.' He pocketed the empty gun. 'Come on. Let's go get Maddie.'

They ran up the stairs.

Halfway up the second flight, a voice brought them to an abrupt halt.

'Stop right there!'

The voice had come from above them.

Maddie and Eddie Stone were at the head of the

stairs. Stone had his arm around Maddie's neck. Ready to squeeze if necessary. Maddie looked frightened but calm.

'Let her go,' Alex called up.

Eddie Stone ignored him. 'Jack!' he called.

'He can't help you,' Danny said.

'Who got shot?' Eddie Stone asked. His voice sounded almost casual. Only Maddie was aware of the tension in his body.

'No one,' said Alex.

'Pity,' Stone said. 'You could have done me a big favour by putting a bullet through Richard Bryson's head.'

'Let the girl go,' Alex called up.

'I don't think so,' said Stone. 'She's going to help me get out of here.' His face was close to hers. His breath on her cheek. 'Isn't that right, Madeleine?'

Danny and Alex glanced at one another. He knew who she was. Not that it mattered much now. Things were on a knife-edge. The time for subterfuge was past.

'We're police officers,' Alex said. 'Release the girl and step away from her.'

Eddie Stone laughed softly. The sound chilled Maddie to the core.

'Will you do something for me?' he called down.

'What?' Danny asked.

'Tell Richard I'll be back later to deal with him.'

With that, Eddie Stone drew away from the edge of the stairs, pulling Maddie with him.

'Follow me, and I'll kill her,' he called down.

He walked her along an upper corridor, his hand gripping the back of her neck. 'I'm sorry,' he said. 'This isn't the way I like to do business. But you can see the situation I'm in.' He looked at her, his ice-blue eyes glittering. 'Those two lads? Are they armed?'

'Yes,' Maddie said, a little too quickly.

'You're not a good liar, Maddie,' said Eddie.

'You can't get away,' Maddie told him.

'So you told me,' said Eddie Stone. 'But I'm not so sure. I know how the police work. They come in mob-handed. They should be swarming all over the house by now. Why aren't they, Maddie? What's going on?' He looked closely at her. 'My guess is that you three are here on your own. Am I right?'

Maddie said nothing as she looked into those cold blue eyes. She had to break away from his stare.

'Oh, so I am right,' Stone whispered. 'Well, well. So, what's Jack Cooper's daughter doing, locked up in my house, pretending to be Grace O'Connor?'

'We're here to get *you*,' Maddie said.

'Is that so?' Eddie smiled grimly. 'I think you've bitten off more than you can chew, Maddie. I think you're in way over your head.'

He opened a door. Maddie found herself in a small utility room. There was a door in the far wall. Eddie shot back the bolts. The door creaked open on to a raised platform of rusted black steel. A fresh breeze blew. Metal stairs zigzagged down the side of the house. A fire escape, leading down into the garden.

The rising sun was bright and bitter in Maddie's eyes as Eddie led her down the creaking steps.

They rounded a corner of the house.

The helicopter stood waiting on the lawn like a gigantic dragonfly.

Eddie's eyes narrowed and his fingers tightened on Maddie's neck. 'Damn!' he whispered.

The pilot was gone.

✪

Mike Evans had been working as a driver and helicopter pilot for Stonecor for six months. He had quickly learned about the underside of the company. The criminal web that stretched across Europe. The web that was now reaching out across the Atlantic. He was paid enough not to care.

But he wasn't paid enough to get himself shot.

No way.

Eddie Stone didn't allow smoking in the house. Mike Evans had ground his cigarette stub out on the lawn. He had walked towards the house, hoping for some coffee. It had been a long night. He'd been on call for twelve hours now – right through those endless negotiations with the Americans.

He had heard Celia Thomson shouting. He had crept warily through to the front of the house. He had heard the single gunshot. That had been enough for him. He had slid back the way he had come. He had sprinted to the end of the garden and gone over the high wall.

Eddie Stone wasn't paying him enough to get shot at.

✖

Danny was the first to make a move. He went slinking up the stairs, pressed to the wall, sure-footed and silent. He snapped a quick glance around the edge of the wall. Maddie and Stone were gone. A door stood open. Danny beckoned to Alex.

They moved cautiously along the passage.

It was a small room. A door gaped, filled with light.

'Fire escape!' Alex said. He ran to the door. Nine metres below him, he could see the foreshortened figures of

Maddie and Eddie Stone moving out into the garden.

He glanced at Danny. 'They're going for the chopper!' he said.

The metal stairs clanged as they pounded down them.

❂

Eddie Stone was in the pilot's seat. Maddie was beside him. In the co-pilot's place. Strapped in.

'It's OK,' Eddie said. 'I've been taking lessons.' His eyes narrowed as he scanned the complex arrangement of switches and levers and dials. He looked at her, grinning savagely. 'Here goes nothing! Hold tight, Maddie! This could be interesting.'

He switched the engine on. The machine shuddered. Above them, the rotor blades began slowly to turn, throwing down long shadows.

Maddie clung to her seat. Petrified. A small voice yelled in her head, as if from a huge distance. *You should do something! You should stop him!*

The shadows of the blades flickered faster and faster, and suddenly there was no shadow at all. The blades had become a continuous grey blur.

Two figures ran from the side of the house. Danny and Alex.

Maddie let out a cry of relief.

Alex pulled out a gun. He stood in front of the helicopter, his legs braced apart, aiming the weapon directly at Eddie Stone.

'I'll only say this once,' he shouted above the roar of the helicopter's engine. 'Turn the motor off or I will open fire on you!'

✪

It was a desperate bluff on Alex's part. Danny knew that. He had seen Alex take out the bullet clip. He knew the gun was empty.

Through the windscreen, he saw hope ignite in Maddie's desperate face. He saw something else in Eddie Stone's expression. Grim, cold determination. It wasn't the look of someone who was about to give himself up.

Stone's arms moved as he engaged the controls.

Alex shouted again. 'This is your last chance!'

The blast of hurricane air from the rotor flung his hollow threat back in his face. Eddie Stone wasn't buying it.

The helicopter lifted from the grass. It shook. The engine snarled and roared. Eddie Stone gave a light touch to the joystick. The helicopter moved cumbersomely forward above the lawn – towards where Alex and Danny were standing.

There was a wild light in Eddie Stone's eyes as he edged the helicopter closer to the two men. The wind tore at their hair and clothes. Maddie saw Danny back off, crouching, his arms flung up across his face. But Alex didn't move. He stood rock-solid as the aircraft bore down on him.

'No!' Maddie shouted. 'Don't!'

Eddie Stone drew back on the joystick. The ground moved suddenly away from them. The rearing back of the big house dropped across the windscreen. There was a shudder. The helicopter banked a little. The tail dipped. Eddie fought the controls to right it.

Maddie closed her eyes. The white wall of the house was horribly close. She felt her stomach turn over.

Stone let out a gust of dry laughter. 'It's OK,' he shouted above the engine noise. 'You can look now. I haven't killed us... yet!'

Maddie opened her eyes. All she could see was blue sky.

Stone eased the joystick and the helicopter made a long, slow curve through the air. The sun flashed briefly in her eyes, before moving around to her left. He adjusted the controls and the helicopter began to fly in a straight line, due south.

Chapter Twenty

As the helicopter lurched towards him, Alex looked straight into Eddie Stone's eyes. He realised in an instant that Stone was prepared to slam the aircraft straight into him. Alex had no bullets in the gun – not that he could have shot at Eddie Stone – not with Maddie in the helicopter beside him.

At the very last second, Alex ducked down, throwing the useless weapon aside. He had failed. Then, a kind of instinct took over. The underside of the black aircraft moved above him. He saw a metal strut. He reached for it. He had no idea what he hoped to do.

As the helicopter lifted, Alex was pulled to his feet,

still clinging to the strut. He pulled upwards and hooked an elbow over the strut. A knee. Then a foot. He looked down. The ground was already ten metres below him.

It flashed through his mind that he must be mad. He saw Danny's face, staring up at him in utter disbelief.

The helicopter turned. Alex tightened his hold. The ground spun under him. He closed his eyes. They were twenty metres in the air now and rising fast. If Alex lost his grip, the fall would kill him. When the helicopter landed, he would be crushed.

Either way, he was dead.

✷

Danny stumbled to his feet – staring up at the black helicopter as it rose with Alex clinging underneath. It had happened so quickly. Danny had thrown himself flat. When he had looked again, it had been to see the black belly of the helicopter hanging over Alex's head. Then Alex had reached up. A moment later and his feet had left the ground.

'Alex stop!'

But it was too late. Alex had managed to get a leg up over the bar to which he was already clinging. The helicopter turned and headed away over the treetops with Alex holding on.

Danny was stunned. Alex and Maddie were gone. His attempt to rescue them had been a disaster. A total disaster.

The helicopter was heading south. Where would that take them? Over the river. Into South West London. Down into Surrey. In twenty minutes, Eddie Stone could be hidden away down there – untraceable.

'No!' Danny ran back to the house. 'That isn't going to happen. He's not going to get away that easily.'

The French windows were unbolted. Danny threw himself into the house. He made his way towards the front of the building. The big thug was still lying unconscious in the hall. He found the woman in the office, by the water dispenser, bathing her head with a wetted tissue.

She shot him a glance of pure loathing.

'I'm a police officer,' Danny said, 'and you're under arrest.'

Celia Thomson gave him a contemptuous look.

The other man was still curled up behind the desk. It didn't look as if he was going to cause any problems for a while.

Danny threw himself into a seat in front of the banks of electronics. He sat there for a moment or two, his eyes raking over the devices. Figuring them out.

Then his hands began to move – turning dials, pulling jack plugs, lowering faders. Once all the heavy duty surveillance and jamming signals had been dampened, Danny reached for a headset and dialled a number on a switchboard.

A female voice answered after two rings.

'Police Investigation Command, how may I help you?'

'Jackie! It's Danny! We've got trouble. Put me through to someone. Quickly.'

'Roland Jakes is here,' Jackie Saunders said. 'I'll patch you through.'

Roland was one of the section leaders. He'd be able to mobilise the troops. The sense of relief made Danny's head spin. Finally, this whole crazy nightmare was going to come to an end.

He heard the sound of the front door closing. He glanced over his shoulder. The woman was gone. He smiled. A rat deserting a sinking ship. No problem. They'd pick her up easily enough later on.

He looked around the room at the banks of filing cabinets and boxes of computer disks.

And if this was what he thought it was, the whole Stonecor empire was about to collapse.

❂

Maddie glanced down. Below them, the rooftops and tight-wound streets of Kensington were rushing by. Away over to her right, she could just see the Hammersmith flyover. Beyond, lay the M4 and Heathrow Airport – where this whole thing had started.

She looked at Eddie Stone. His eyebrows were knitted in the effort of piloting the aircraft. He confused her. He didn't look like her idea of a criminal. He seemed the kind of guy you might meet at Quaglino's. The kind of guy you might want to dance with. To take home to meet your folks.

Maddie shivered. Sweet face – cold eyes. Easy smile – hard heart.

'Why are you staring at me?' he asked, his voice raised against the noise of the engine. Maddie hadn't even realised that he'd been aware of her eyes on him.

'I'm wondering about you,' she said. 'I'm thinking about what kind of person you are.'

'Ahh.'

There was a pause.

'Where are you taking me?' Maddie asked.

'I don't know yet,' Eddie Stone replied. He shot her a quick look. 'I needed to get out of there. I thought they'd be less likely to give me trouble if I had you with me.' He frowned, and then smiled his easy, sweet smile. 'You've given me some problems, Maddie Cooper. Serious problems.'

'Good.'

His eyebrows lifted as he looked at her. 'You're a cool kid,' he said.

'I'm not a kid,' Maddie said. 'My mother was killed. My father was crippled. I had to grow up pretty quickly.'

'And you got a bullet in the left side of your pelvis,' Eddie Stone said. 'Which meant that you had to kiss your dancing career goodbye.' Maddie was shocked that he knew those details.

He gave her another smile. 'I followed the news, Maddie. It was an unfortunate business – shooting people down in the street. That's far too public. It's messy. Old-fashioned.' He shook his head. 'That's not the way to solve problems.'

'So, what would you have done?' Maddie asked coldly.

'Me?' He flashed her another ice-blue glance. 'I wouldn't have put myself in that position in the first place. It doesn't make good business sense.'

A wave of sickness came over Maddie. 'Your father tried to kill my whole family,' she choked. 'And you talk about it as if it was just a bad business decision!'

201

He reached out and briefly touched her arm. His fingers were warm. 'It's OK,' he said. 'Take deep breaths, Maddie. Don't lose it.'

It was weird, listening to him. His voice was so calm – so reasonable.

'You have to understand something,' he said as the black helicopter flew above the crowded streets of Chelsea. 'The family business always comes first. Anything or anyone who threatens it has to be dealt with. It's unfortunate – but that's the real world, Maddie. That's the way things work. Your father knew that. He knew the risk he was taking.' A bleak smile lifted the side of his mouth. 'It's all to do with cause and effect, Maddie. You push someone, and they're going to push back. That's life. And don't kid yourself, Maddie – our fathers are just two sides of the same coin. They both do what it takes to get the job done.'

'That's the most ridiculous thing I've ever heard!' Maddie said. 'You're nothing like my father! You frighten people. You hurt people.' Her voice rose. 'You destroy people's lives.'

'Only if I have to, Maddie,' he said calmly. 'Only if I have to.'

✖

The rushing wind was cold and cruel. It gnawed at Alex's fingers, buffeting him, clawing at him, as if trying to rip him from his precarious hold under the helicopter. His hands were growing numb. His head was full of a rushing, roaring noise that made it impossible for him to think. Every tensed muscle in his body ached.

It might almost be worth the deadly fall, just to stop the agony in his cramped legs and arms. He gritted his teeth.

He knew he would not be able to hold on for much longer. Another few minutes and the decision would be made for him. His icy fingers would lose their grip. He would fall to his death.

✪

Now the helicopter was flying over the thin brown streak of Chelsea Creek. Ahead, Maddie saw the arching curve of the Thames, crossed by the Battersea railway bridge. She saw Chelsea Harbour Pier and the dark wharves on the far bank. The river was at low tide – banks of mud and shingle showed on either side of the narrowed strip of gliding brown water.

Beyond the river, the suburbs of South West London spread to a hazy blue horizon.

'You should give up,' Maddie said. 'You can't carry

203

on pretending to be running a legitimate business after this. Everyone's going to know you're a crook.'

'Don't worry about me,' Eddie Stone said. 'I'll survive.' He looked at her. 'Tell me – I know Richard Bryson is all front and no brains – but how did you convince him that you were Grace O'Connor? How did you plan all this out?'

Maddie said nothing.

Stone gave a bark of laughter. 'You didn't plan it at all!' he said. 'You just stumbled into it by accident. Richard was setting something up with O'Connor's daughter, and the three of you just got lucky.' Eddie Stone's shrewd guesses were disconcerting. 'What was it?' he asked. 'Some kind of training exercise? Grace O'Connor must have flown into Heathrow. You were there, weren't you? The three of you. And you decided to go for it.' His eyes gleamed. 'My God, Maddie – you're something else.'

'It was worth it,' she said. 'Whatever you do to me, it was worth it, because we've made sure you're finished.'

Eddie Stone laughed again. 'Don't you believe it, Maddie. You've given me some headaches – but do you really think I'm stupid enough to keep everything in one house?' He shook his head. 'No, I'm sorry,

Maddie. It's not that easy. I'm nowhere near finished – not by a long way.'

'My father won't rest until he finds me,' Maddie said.

Eddie Stone's response chilled Maddie to the heart.

'Who says he's going to find you?'

Chapter Twenty•One

Maddie's heart was hammering. 'Are you going to kill me?' she asked.

A pained look flashed over Eddie Stone's face. 'What put that idea into your head, Maddie?' He looked at her – smiling. Easy smile – hard heart. 'Of course I'm not going to kill you.'

As Maddie looked into those frozen blue eyes, she knew he was lying.

The helicopter flew out over the Thames.

Maddie had two choices: either to give in, or to fight back.

But what could she do? Eddie Stone was in control – any action she took would imperil both of them.

Unless she could jump clear while they were over the water.

She moved her hand to the door.

'Central locking, Maddie,' Eddie said calmly. 'You won't be able to get it open. Sorry.'

A kind of wild desperation flowed through Maddie. For a few crazy moments she didn't care what happened to her – she just had to do something to silence his voice – something that would hurt him as much as his family had hurt her.

She jack-knifed her legs, bunching her muscles and twisting in her seat. She kicked out towards the dashboard with both feet. She had no thought in her head other than the desire to bring the helicopter down and put an end to this whole terrible ordeal.

Eddie let out a shout of alarm and anger as Maddie's feet smashed into the controls of the helicopter. But he was too late. The damage had been done.

The turbine engine Jetranger helicopter has a switch-off valve – a red switch located on the bank in front of the pilot. It cuts off the fuel. The heel of Maddie's right foot came hammering down on the red switch – engaging it and breaking it off in one movement. Sparks fizzed and flew from the control panel.

'You stupid fool!' Eddie wrenched at the joystick. The helicopter shuddered and began to keel over in the air. The engine was starved of fuel. The rotors began to slow.

'Don't take it personally, Eddie.' Maddie's eyes were cold. 'It was just a business decision.'

Eddie gave her a single look of uncontrolled rage. The helicopter was falling. There was nothing he could do to keep it in the air.

Maddie hardly had time to comprehend what happened next. Eddie Stone threw himself against the door. The door burst open. He tumbled out. The helicopter swung and bucked as it plunged towards the river.

With an incoherent scream of terror, Maddie lurched over to the joystick.

○

Alex was in agony. His fingers were slipping. He was seconds away from falling. The noise of the engines was deafening. The wind was blasting in his face – making it impossible for him to open his eyes. He was unaware that the murky brown waters of the Thames were flowing beneath him.

The sound changed suddenly. The engine howled and coughed and went silent. The bulk of the helicopter became a dead weight above him. Something had gone terribly wrong.

He prised his eyes open, finally seeing where they were. The helicopter was plunging towards the water. When it hit, it's weight would kill him. Then he saw something fall from the side of the stricken machine. A man. Jumping from the helicopter – tumbling helplessly down towards the water.

Alex only had a fraction of a second to act. He let his legs fall from the strut. He hung for a moment, full stretch from the underside of the helicopter. He fully expected to be dead in the next few seconds. He let go and knifed down into the river. The cold water sheathed him in a foam of rushing bubbles.

He kicked out and fought the water with his arms. Blinded. His ears full of the rush of his descent. He held his breath. Still going down. Entombed in swirling dark water. The coldness slashed him like razors. It made him want to gasp with the pain. To suck in water. To drown and be done with it.

✪

The helicopter went into auto rotation – its rapid descent keeping the air flowing through the rotor blades – keeping them spinning for a few precious seconds.

Maddie gripped the joystick with both hands, leaning – stretched out across the helicopter – fighting to keep the aircraft level. She was aware of the ground rushing up. Too fast. Far too fast. The high embankment filled the windscreen.

The impact shook her hands free of the joystick. She was thrown about in the cockpit like a rag doll. All she saw in those few dreadful moments was a great fountain of water that jetted up all around her. Water flooded in through the open door. Icy and cruel.

The helicopter lurched to one side and became still.

Maddie panicked, struggling to get herself free from the seat belt that pinned her inside the cockpit. Then she realised that the helicopter wasn't sinking. It stood at a crazy angle, dark water lapping in through the open door.

In a kind of dream, Maddie wrenched herself free of her seatbelt. She fell across the cockpit and slithered into the freezing water. It made her gasp and cry out. But it wasn't deep. Mud sucked at her legs as she struggled to her feet.

She had managed to bring the helicopter down in shallow water. The bank was only a couple of metres away. She waded ashore, laughing wildly. Exhausted. Stunned. She fell to her knees in the thick

Thames mud. She coughed. She had swallowed water.

She clawed her way on to firmer ground and fell on to her face with a groan.

'Maddie? Maddie? Are you OK?'

Strong hands turned her on to her back. She struggled and retched.

'No! No! Get away from me!'

'Maddie! It's OK! It's me.'

She opened her eyes. Alex was leaning over her. Except that it was impossible.

She stared up at him. Water was pouring off him. He looked exhausted.

'How... did you get here... so quick...?' she gasped.

'I hitched a lift.' He spluttered, coughing up river water. He fell down by her side. For a few moments they lay side by side on the shingle bank of the river, staring up into the clear blue sky.

Their ordeal was over.

✪

Police launches prowled the stretch of the Thames that lay between Battersea and Wandsworth Bridges like hounds on the scent. Half a dozen police cars lined the embankment at Chelsea Harbour. Maddie was sitting sideways on the back seat of one of the cars, with her feet out in the street. She was wrapped

in a blanket. Sipping scalding coffee. Shivering.

Uniformed and plain-clothes officers were standing against the sun. From where she was sitting, Maddie could see the sagging rotors at an odd angle as the helicopter settled deeper into the Thames mud.

Danny was there. And Alex, his broad shoulders covered by a blanket, his hair wet and dark over his forehead.

A special search team was operating out in the middle of the river. Frogmen were diving and surfacing.

Alex jumped down off the low wall and walked back to where Maddie was sitting. He cradled a mug of steaming coffee in both hands.

She looked up at him. 'Anything?' she asked.

He shook his head. 'Not so far.' He glanced towards the river. 'They don't think he could have survived. It's too cold out there. And he had that heavy coat on. It would have dragged him down.'

Maddie closed her eyes. She saw Eddie Stone's smiling face in her mind. Smiling up at her through six metres of murky water. She shuddered. 'They think he's dead, then?'

'It looks like it.'

Maddie sighed. She looked up at Alex. 'This wasn't how I imagined it ending at all,' she said. She gave him a brave smile. 'I can't decide whether we won or lost.'

Danny came up behind Alex. 'I think we won,' he said. 'There's a team heading over to the house in Addison Road. Once they've checked out all those hard drives and optical disks, I think Stonecor will be history.'

Maddie frowned. 'Eddie said there was more,' she said. 'In other places.'

Danny looked over his shoulder at the cold river. 'Yeah, well – maybe so. But it isn't going to do him much good where he is.'

Maddie stood up. She walked towards the river. She stood staring down into the slow flow of the oily water.

Was Eddie Stone really dead? It was hard to take in.

A voice shouted. 'Excuse me – Miss Cooper?' Maddie turned. An officer stood by a patrol car. He held up a phone. 'Call for you.'

She turned her back to the river. She pulled a hank of wet hair off her face.

'It's the DCS,' said the officer.

Maddie blinked at him. Who? Then it dawned on her what he meant. 'Dad?'

The officer nodded, handing her the phone. A priority call from PIC Control had gone through to Jack Cooper –

alerting him to the situation. He had wasted no time in asking to be patched through to his daughter.

She held the phone to her ear. 'Er... Hello Dad,' she said. 'It's me. I'm OK. We're all OK.' She suddenly felt weak and worn to shreds and dead on her feet. She leaned against the side of the car, tightly clutching on to the lifeline of the phone.

'Dad?' she whispered. 'When are you coming home?'

✪

Maddie, Alex and Danny sat outside Jack Cooper's office – waiting to be called in. Tara Moon was leaning against her desk, arms folded, head tilted, eyebrows raised.

'They found his coat,' Alex said. 'When the tide turned, they hoicked it out of the water at Chelsea Reach.' He was talking about Eddie Stone.

'He wasn't in it,' Danny added. 'Which was a real shame, if you ask me.' Tara smiled.

'They think he drowned,' Alex said. He glanced at Maddie. 'Although not everyone agrees with them.'

'I'll believe it when they find him,' she said. 'Not before.'

'The tide was going out,' Danny said. 'It would have swept him downstream. The body could be halfway to France by now.'

'Or he could have swum to safety,' Maddie persisted. 'Alex did.'

She couldn't get Eddie Stone's face out of her head. She felt haunted by him. She would catch herself glancing up at odd times – expecting to see him standing there watching her. Smiling at her. When the phone rang, she was almost afraid to pick up in case it was his voice at the other end.

It was the day after the helicopter had crashed into the Thames.

DCS Cooper and his assistant had returned early from the Economic Summit. The Eddie Stone situation overrode everything else.

Jack Cooper's first concern on arriving in London had been for Maddie's safety. She had been wary – expecting an explosion of anger. But Jack Cooper was too relieved to be angry. Father and daughter had clung together.

He had insisted that Maddie was checked out by a police doctor. She had been pronounced fit and well – but physically and emotionally wiped out. She had crashed out within minutes of getting home that afternoon. She had slept for ten hours. Utterly spent.

The following morning, Maddie, Danny and Alex had been ordered to write full reports of the incident.

215

Now they were waiting. Uneasily.

The intercom sounded. Tara Moon leaned back over her desk and flicked a switch. 'Yes, sir?'

'Send them in, please.' Jack Cooper's voice was curt.

Tara hooked her head towards the door.

Maddie, Alex and Danny looked at one another. Alex was the first to get up.

As they walked into Jack Cooper's office, Tara Moon rattled her fingers on the desk top in a slow, sinister drumbeat. The accompaniment of victims to the execution block.

Danny glanced back at her. 'Funnee-ee!' he whispered.

She winked at him as she closed the door on them.

Jack Cooper was behind his desk. Their reports were spread out in front of him. He was frowning.

'They make interesting reading,' he growled. 'You did some quick thinking out there.' His eyes moved from face to face. From Danny to Maddie to Alex. 'You kept your heads in difficult circumstances. Things could have got a lot worse.' His dark eyes glittered. 'I hope you've learned some important lessons.'

'You bet,' said Danny. Cooper stopped him with a look. 'Sorry, boss.'

'Under the circumstances,' Jack Cooper continued, 'I'm prepared to overlook the fact that you acted without orders. You saw an opportunity to do some good work, and you took that opportunity.' His eyes roamed their faces again. 'Mistakes were made,' he said. 'I've attached some comments to your reports. I expect you to read and digest.'

His hand came to rest on a closely printed sheet of paper. Not one of their reports. Some kind of official document, Maddie assumed.

Jack Cooper leaned back in his wheelchair. 'Eddie Stone's body still hasn't been found,' he said. 'So we have to accept the fact that he may have survived the fall. I've been in touch with the Home Secretary, and Michael Stone is going to be informed of the situation.'

Maddie said, 'I guess he knows already. He won't be happy. We should watch out for some kind of retaliation.'

'Are they in a position to retaliate?' Alex asked.

'Possibly,' Jack Cooper said. 'If we take what Eddie Stone said to Maddie at face value, then we can't assume that Stonecor has been completely eradicated. We've dealt them a serious blow, that much is certain. The house in Holland Park is offering up a huge amount of important information, and Bryson is proving very helpful with our enquiries.'

'Have they found Celia yet?' Maddie asked. 'She was the ice queen from hell.'

'She hasn't turned up yet,' said Jack Cooper. 'But we're picking up other Stonecor employees all over the city.' He smiled for the first time. 'That was a good day's work, people. I'm proud of you.'

'What's happened to Grace and her boyfriend?' Maddie asked.

'They've been sent back to Boston,' said her father. 'No doubt Patrick O'Connor will give them a warm welcome when they arrive. But at least he'll get his diamonds and his daughter back intact.' He looked at Maddie. 'Although, if he's any kind of man, the safe return of his daughter will be all that concerns him.'

Maddie smiled.

Jack Cooper picked up the printed document from his desk. He sat looking at it for a few moments. Maddie glanced at Alex and Danny – they were all wondering if their interview was at an end.

Jack Cooper leaned forwards, pushing the document across his desk.

'I want you to read this, Maddie,' he said.

She picked it up. 'What is it?'

'It's the Official Secrets Act,' Jack Cooper said.

'You'll have to sign it if you want to become a full-time PIC trainee.'

Maddie stared at the document. She looked at her father. His face was impassive. Danny was grinning. Alex was looking closely at her.

'Anyone got a pen?' she asked.

'Way to go, Maddie!' said Danny, handing her his.

'I hope you understand the serious nature of what you are committing yourself to, Maddie,' said Jack Cooper. 'You'll be on an equal footing with Danny and Alex. You'll get no preferential treatment. The three of you showed strong teamwork in all of this, and I'm sure there will be other opportunities for you to work together.' His eyes gleamed. 'Less dangerous opportunities, that is.' He took the signed document from Maddie and closed it into a folder. 'Dismissed,' he said.

They left his office. Maddie felt a bit dazed by the sudden turn of events. She hadn't been expecting anything so thrilling as becoming a PIC trainee. It had taken her breath away.

Tara Moon looked up from her desk.

'How did it go?' she asked.

'I'm on the team,' Maddie said dazedly. 'I can hardly believe it! I've just signed up! The boss says the

three of us will be able to work together again.'

'So, I guess that makes us officially partners,' Danny said, grinning at Maddie and Alex.

'Yes,' said Alex with a smile. 'Partners in crime!'

SPECIAL AGENTS
FINAL SHOT

A death threat hangs over Britain's tennis ace

It's a week before the Wimbledon Tennis
Championships and all eyes are on British hopeful,
Will Anderson. But when a murder investigation
leads police to a stash of mutilated photographs
of Will, it becomes horribly clear that he is
the murderer's next victim.

When police Investigation Squad trainees, Alex,
Danny and Maddie go undercover with Will,
things turn nasty.

Alex, Danny and Maddie – three teenagers fighting
crime on the streets of London.

0-00-714844-5

HarperCollins *Children's Books*